PENGUIN BOOKS
PRIVATE – DO NOT OPEN

Sasha Soldatow was born in Plochingen, Germany, in 1947, the son of Russian parents. He arrived in Melbourne in 1949 where he studied music and history. In 1972 he moved to Sydney, attracted by its libertarian-anarchist tradition. *Politics of the Olympics* was published in 1980. Sasha Soldatow has also written and performed many one-man theatre pieces including a renowned fragment on Percy Grainger. He is represented in the Australian National Gallery.

D1547681

PRIVATE –
DO NOT OPEN

SASHA SOLDATOW

PENGUIN BOOKS
assisted by the Literature Board of the Australia Council

Penguin Books Australia Ltd,
487 Maroondah Highway, PO Box 257
Ringwood, Victoria 3134, Australia
Penguin Books Ltd,
Harmondsworth, Middlesex, England
Penguin Books,
40 West 23rd Street, New York, NY 10010, USA
Penguin Books Canada Limited,
2801 John Street, Markham, Ontario, Canada L3R IB4
Penguin Books (NZ) Ltd,
182–190 Wairau Road, Auckland 10, New Zealand

First published by Penguin Books Australia, 1987

Typeset in 10pt Century Light by Dovatype, Melbourne
Made and printed in Australia by The Book Printer, Maryborough, Victoria

CIP

Soldatow, Sasha 1947–
   Private – do not open.

   ISBN 0 14 008526 2.

   I. Title.

A823'.3

Creative writing program assisted by the Literature Board
of the Australia Council, the Federal Government's arts
funding and advisory body.

Author's note: This book was written without the assistance
of the Literature Board of the Australia Council.
My thanks to Bruce Sims for pulling it together.

CONTENTS

'Life ten years ago, was largely
a personal matter.'

F. Scott Fitzgerald, *The Crack-up*.

PRACTISING **D**YING

PRACTISING DYING

What were the faces that my mother would have seen during the war when she was a nurse in a German field hospital? A prisoner and a hated Russian, she was evacuated to help the wounded but mostly the dying. Boys, as she calls them (for remember she is a mother). Boys arriving by the truckload, injured and sick with gangrene and shock. Boy soldiers contorted and twisted by the impact of what they had just come through, knowing the immediacy of what had been done to them.

They would come in their endless convoys and she would take them in. Knowing there was no more medicine. Knowing they were critical for help. Knowing they were dying. Knowing that of twenty that arrived in the night, eighteen would be dead in the morning.

Typhoid. Deadly in its delirium, typhoid was there with

them, hanging over their heads in a million exploding cells. And nothing to be done except to soothe a fever, listen to the ravings about parents and lovers, children, wives, homes, endless homes. Endless countries of belonging that were too deep to obliterate from the mind. All this she would strain to wipe away, hopelessly, hour for hour, into the weeks of nights of tiredness.

And the soldiers would pinch her skin. With their last strength they would remember what they were fighting for. Their instincts tottering, it would still burst through, this need to destroy. It would make valiant forays into the outside which was quickly becoming furry with unconsciousness. But they fought. How they fought. With every last ascent they would return to the cause. For they were men. And they were men at war. And their inhumanity was the rage they lived by. So they told her, 'You dirty Russian pig. You scum. I will kill you. I will wipe you off the face of the earth. I will pull your skin off with my bare hands.' They dug their nails into the woman who was their only contact with a different kind of world. And she, pinched and bruised, she never recounts what went through her mind. She only speaks of how she would see them dead the next morning, and another truckload arriving. She was twenty.

———————

Outside my window, smoke streams from the chimneys into the early morning air far off in Botany Bay on the horizon. The night is so still that the smoke is hardly touched by any breeze. It's as if the thousands of people asleep between me and this horizon have ceased to exist.

Sitting by the open window I think of the people I've been with and the places I've known in my life. I down a coffee to keep me going and another brandy for the late hour. My head is already drunk tonight. It will be sore again tomorrow morning. Drunkedness. That exquisite window on your own world. Life in all its tenderness. And the chimneys spitting pollution reminding me of self-indulgence.

This lasting window on the world beyond slowly enlarges as I look outside, looking beyond the chimneys into a clean night. There's nothing like a drunk romantic haze to keep you up, a very late night with bacon and eggs to look forward to in the morning. And coffee. And an aspirin. But it's still night, this night to fill in before breakfast. A night glittering across the million lights wide awake, electrically awake, the soul of modernism lighting up my insomnia.

Like the people I've known. Countless thousands. Friends for a moment or for eternity. The criss-cross connection of parties. The ends of a night. A taxi home, loose change, the farewells, the goodbyes, semi-sleeping, tired, and a last cigarette, lit but never smoked all the way through, in one's own bed, one's own world, in tomorrow.

But the night is yet young when you're drunk but not tired enough to stop drinking. And the friends to remember in the morning with black coffee and bacon and eggs are still with you, if only in conversation.

When I wake tomorrow, the morning will of course start with abrupt rebellion. The shock of waking up feeling like death. By noon the hangover will become a wish to live. By lunchtime only greasy food interests you. So you eat, eat and smoke, smoke and drink anything that comes your way. Such is the story of inner-city living. That and a desire to be modern, to live through another day. But when evening draws near, even before that, at four o'clock, a full heart races to remind you that the indifferences of daytime cannot continue.

The people you've been with and the people you've known come back to involve you again. They crowd the pavement as your taxi pulls out. You catch them looking as the cab swerves.

5

As you ride they holler in the dusk, try to wave you down. Evening reminds you of their presence.

Some have stories that stretch back in time. They are the lucky ones who have survived to spell out the past. Nothing shores the memory like survival.

Moving out along the street, passing houses in a car, you listen to the past, the links that connect a suburb to a house to a person, a happening. Someone lived there. There, that's the house. No, it's the next one. It's hard to tell, everything changes so quickly.

No one lives there anymore except people we don't know who have lock-controlled doors and a living space like in New York. Where we all once lived in poverty with open doors and where people we remember by name lived before us, they are now apartments indistinguishable from the history of the world over the last twenty years – New York, Paris, London, Ontario, Sydney. It's all the same now.

'Living somewhere has its advantages,' says the taxi driver.

'And everything can so easily become traumatic.'

'Your emotions,' says the taxi driver. 'You have a fine control over them. But they're so powerful, they're killers. Where are you going?'

'To a flat in Kings Cross. It's my last chance for a love affair.'

'You must be kidding. When you lie to yourself you only make things worse. Because others then think you're lying to them too. You say, if only this would come true!' The taxi turns a corner roughly then straightens out. 'And when it doesn't,' the driver continues, 'you say, that was my last chance. Well, it was your second-last chance. In life all chances are the one before the end. Whereabouts in Kings Cross?'

'Oak Lane,' you say. 'Another party.'

'That's in Potts Point.'

The taxi creeps up Darlinghurst Road, the heart of the Cross, packed out on Saturday night. Full of men bemoaning their fate, young louts, prostitutes on heroin and fifty-year-old lust-driven women. Everyone else is just looking. At the spruikers lying about live sex acts on stage, hoods in ice-cream parlours, coffee shops with windows facing the street, fast-food joints, illegal watch-sellers, drunk buskers and fortune-tellers. Irene will read your fate – three dollars for a short reading, five dollars for half an hour in McDonalds. At the end of your fortune you cannot help yourself. You say, like everyone else does, 'Goodnight, Irene.'

The taxi pauses in a traffic jam just outside where the christians haunt the street. REPENT NOW, says the sign. Across the road a lone atheist tells another version. 'To die is not to sleep. To die is not to go to an everlasting dream and be reborn. To die is first to be bed-ridden, a disaster of being tended to with no legs, or half a stomach, or no speech. That's modern death. It is to be smothered in deluxe astringent surroundings being fed medical crap through a tube while waiting for the final blood spurt out of your nostrils and anus while the *Te Deum* is being piped through the Muzak machine.' The taxi moves on.

'You can be dead at thirty,' says the driver. 'You can spend your whole life waiting for true romantic death and yet be dead all that time.' The taxi pauses at the lights.

'At forty it's a bit more gruesome. Jumping under a train or off a bridge saying, why did I do it? No one ever knows what they mean.' The cab starts again.

'Or a drug overdose or a car accident,' continues the driver. 'Forty is like twenty in a way. Except older. There's something about doubling.' We are now in Macleay Street.

'At fifty, when the intimations of mortality are near but you are healthy but no longer young, cars and trains assume a different aspect. They seem too slow. At fifty you look forward to a hundred. And you start to look back in a different way.'

'At a hundred I'll want to live forever and know everyone,' you say. The driver laughs.

''That's the lie, isn't it. To live till a hundred and then forever.' Then the reflective voice returns. 'But there's all that time before you reach a hundred. At ninety you resent the living. At eighty you actually recall sexual pleasure. And at seventy you wonder, heartbroken, where it all went. Seventy is like seventeen. Both of those ages are a kind of celebration. You have foiled death for a moment. Seventeen and seventy are both symbols of clinging on. Fifty is the turning point.'

We pull up at the party and I pay the driver who counts out my change. 'Death is no adventure. It is forced on people. I don't know what happens at sixty. I've got two years to go. I'll let you know.' The taxi drives away leaving me at my party. The chimneys at Botany Bay are spewing out their pollution as I press the buzzer and Joanna lets me in.

He is like a guitar riff. He is unashamedly attractive. Anything suits him. Like his short hair, his ear-ring and his Aboriginal tattoo.

He is the boy-figure, more attractive because he is twenty-four.

He runs away, appears, disappears, is gone, then around, then gone again, missing, sniffing amyl, snorting coke, mixing orgasms.

He leans on you. Lucky you.

'Compare us,' he says of his high school friend. 'We're both the same age but which of us looks younger?'

It is an unfair question to ask me. I identify with them both. This dropout idealist who wants to work in Nicaragua but speaks no Spanish. It's as if the revolutionary spirit of the International Brigade still lives. And then there's his high school friend who is like a soul possessed. Who identifies with the dissolute dramatic undercurrents of Soviet communism to the extent that he will seek out seedy Romanian and Yugoslav bars in the back streets of Newtown and St Peters, eating offal and drinking beer and slivovitz among tables of solitary immigrants crying into their overpriced drinks. Thinking of Guy Burgess and Leningrad, of Moscow toilets and Bratsk, the hydroelectric gay city of the New Future.

'You both live at the same pace,' I say.

'Yes, but one of us does look younger.' He smiles easily, without trying. Drugs make him look beautiful. Drugs relocate his desires. Drugs and pop music. You can never say no. He never says yes. Yet he promises everything. To you, to everyone.

'You must admit I look younger.'

'Naive sailors have better lines,' I say, with no sincerity. 'Especially at parties.'

'It shouldn't have happened,' he says. 'Sleeping with you. It wasn't meant to happen, I didn't have a clue who I was with.'

'That's a big fib,' I say, but he has disappeared again. He has gone to pick up a twilight date.

'That'd be right,' says his older-looking same-age friend. 'He really gets out of it. He probably wouldn't have known who it was.'

'That doesn't wash with me,' I say. 'I was there.'

(There is often a need to deny everything, but I like people who don't apologise.)

It is impossible to tell it like it happens.

In his late thirties he started hanging around with eighteen-year-old guys from England. He was twice as old as most of them, older in some cases than their fathers. They all felt this difference in age although in most cases it didn't matter nearly as much as any of them had imagined.

Andrew and I go to the country. Andrew is my friend. He travels in and out of my life as good friends do. We are going away because he is going overseas. For good. I have a spare bed made up for him. That is the unspoken deference to our continuing friendship. I love him. I am thirty-seven, he is twenty-two. He is not my lover nor is he my son. It is hard to describe what he means to me. It is enough to say that telling this, like this, in a story, is a gift to him. I am trying to be honest.

Sometimes it worried him when he thought he was just hanging out after the new. Chasing young cock. Not that he'd fucked with many of them and then not often.

I first noticed this other man when Andrew and I changed for the bus at Woodend. He sat behind Andrew. I sat on the other side of the aisle. I think he noticed me too, though I cannot confirm this.

He looked familiar. I will explain what I mean by that last remark. He had not shaved for three days. He had gentle eyes. He was disorganised. His hair was just begining to grey. He had that merry look that heavy drinkers sometimes enjoy. I could feel him looking at me when I tried not to look at him. I liked him immediately. He was my age.

Andrew and I passed cigarettes between us. This man kept glancing. Andrew was not at this stage aware of this other man. This renegade. This survivor. This familiar stranger.

On those occasions when he noticed, and it wasn't a shock of recognition, it was something gentler and more worldly, at those times he noticed that their bodies were smoother, more tapered, not surprisingly more boyish. Sleeping with them, he rediscovered, was more than sharing a bed. It was more like being tucked in for the night. Not the messy disturbance of lovers. But it wasn't like being young again either. Not at all.

(There are moments in life, impulsive moments, which one should never let pass. These are the moments that save lives. To react in these moments is to take a chance. That is the only way one can live without regrets.)

So this is how it happened next. Andrew and I got off the bus in Daylesford. We were on the main street, walking. The other man stayed on the other side of the road, dawdling, looking in windows. My chances were ebbing. I could not lose the moment.

'Are you lost?'

'I'm looking for the taxi. It should be here, there's only one in this town and it always meets the bus.' You then walked across the road to join us.

'You look familiar,' I said. 'Have we met before? It would have been a long time ago. In Melbourne. There's something about you. Do you remember me?'

After the funeral of someone he knew, he'd felt very removed from all these middle-aged mourners, his friends. He was now an old hand at handling death. It was beginning to touch him more often as he grew older. So, instinctively, he turned away from those whose experience of people disappearing forever had become as protectively dulled as his own, and turned instead to a kid, one of his eighteen-year-olds for whom it was still novel and raw, a frightening suspension, the first scar. He checked his response against his.

(There are people I know who have given up drinking. It is hard to talk to them. They are never unpredictable. They think too much. They have become scared of the spontaneity of drunkedness and its after-effects. He was not like this.)

'We would've got drunk together,' I said to you.

'That'd be right,' you replied.

'Want to come over for a drink? I've got scotch and vodka.'

'Sure,' you said. 'I'm Irish.'

'So am I,' said Andrew.

Some would say that sexual preference starts with mutual attraction. I deny that now. It starts with kissing. Deep tongue kissing. Fecund kissing. Deep sucking, longing for more. No awareness, no regrets. A something nothing. A blasphemous need. No one being anyone. No surprises, no shocks. Kidding each other. A big joke. Champagne kisses.

11

Rich kisses. Kisses like a fart. The smell of another's being.

'I don't know if you know it and I don't know if I can describe it accurately. I don't even know if I understand it properly myself, but there's a smell. And a taste. They're much the same really. It's an awareness.'

(Andrew has gone to bed. I am alone with Terry. The scotch has been drunk. We are drinking the vodka. We have also kissed each other. It is now no longer a matter of time.)

'The first time it happened was the first time I fell in love. It doesn't happen with everyone. It's the special people, after your first fuck with them. And it only lasts about three days.

'It is so vivid. The memory is as strong as when you're feeling it. It's not during fucking. It comes after. It's hard to explain. It comes afterwards, later, the next morning, but not immediately the next morning. And for the next few days it is the taste and smell of another man. Everything smells of him. And the taste is of him on your tongue.'

(Terry and I are already on each other's breath like mist.)

'It's the taste of another person. I can't explain it. It's like suddenly being taken over, becoming made different. Then after a couple of days you just don't notice anymore.' (In bed that night we hold each other like two grown men do. I will tell you how that is later.)

He felt my arse with his finger. I moved my legs so he could touch me better. He pushed his finger in. The arse only contracts momentarily on penetration. Then it opens, like waking up, like a yawn.

'I'd introduce you both to each other,' Terry says next morning. 'But you'd get an awful reaction from my lover. He'd want to know what you wanted from me. He'd assume I was fucking you.'

'Well, you are.'

Terry looks and smiles, his eyes grinning. 'That's what I mean.'

'You could say I was looking for companionship.'

'He'd say you were old enough to look after yourself.'

He spat on my arse. The moment before you are fucked, that split second before his cock enters you, that is the most dangerous of moments. You must prepare yourself, be ready, expect the momentary seizure of this violation. The body will tighten at this foreign intrusion, then everything is well. Your arse will lie open for as long as is needed.

'Have you ever wanted to settle down and live with anyone?' You can tell that Andrew and I are friends because we talk a lot, walk and talk, drink and talk. You can tell Andrew and I are friends because often when we are together we are mute with silence.

'Terry's been with this guy for nine years. It's interesting that he told me that they didn't fuck much anymore, that if things didn't improve they'd split up. And then he told you something completely different. Rough fucking in the afternoon. Bum scratching.'

'I'd like to live with someone, but I've never met the right person,' says Andrew after we've walked for a while.

'You're not desperate enough.'

'I am. But it's not a matter of desperation.'

'It is if you want it badly enough. You'd take almost anyone.'

'No you don't. You wait.'

If I lie here on my bed very quietly, not moving, breathing silently, I might hear a car turn the corner. I might hear it continue up my street and stop. I might hear the click of the handbrake. I might hear the door open and close. And then there will be a silence while the world pauses and stops. Then I might hear footsteps and a voice. And my heart will race without control until the doorbell startles me because I am expecting it. And I will answer it because it might be the person I am not expecting. And I won't know what to do because I know it will be him.

Terry and Andrew have gone back to Melbourne. I have stayed in Daylesford to finish this story about falling in love.

I must write it quickly before the traces of some tastes and smells vanish.

If he does not come before seven o'clock, then he will not come. It is now six twenty-four. I must sit by the window and watch.

Listen Terry, I must be quick. My arse keeps on reminding me and I must write this down before my body heals the memory. You fucked me. The beer I'm drinking tastes of your hair. We walked and talked. It still hasn't rained. The dust on the tracks smells of your balls. I have your address in my pocket. And I know the difference between a young man's body and yours.

We both know that life is only worth a moment.

HASS STORY

EARLY MORNING, DAYLESFORD

A motor car passes by on some potato paddock back street somewhere far away. The chimney focuses its noise through the trees to within three feet of where I'm lying. The car has little relevance to my story except that it intrudes into my awareness at this four o'clock night hour of silence. It enters and vanishes without leaving any inspiration. Except for a dream memory it has nothing to do with me except its interruption wakes me and takes me outside the warm blankets of a double bed.

I am alone.

I lie suspended in the night ceiling.

For a moment I listen to my night thoughts. Crystallising outside the house, they wander into the garden which is frozen with motion, into the fir trees creaking with restlessness, and further still into the Jim Crow Ranges where my thought crystals dance and crackle and grow and multiply into things I can no longer feel in thoughts.

I lie wandering in the subcutaneous layers of myself. I am dreaming thoughts and feeling out patterns in my living. I am releasing experiences into my mindstream, experiences in sequences that only I and no one else can ever know.

Experiences of my loving that are comparisons. Bits of sentences to and from people. Archaic gestures towards emotions. Leaving lovers. Being left. Speaking thoughts that are forgotten. Having a conversation on a night of rain. Freaking out on paranoia. Being rescued. Getting drunk. Losing my glasses, my cool. Walking out angry. Screaming. Saying I'm sorry.

These things are kept, all of them. They keep recurring. They hide during the day but emerge at night. Stealthily they creep out of their corners and occupy my mind with people and belongings and events. They populate me and I recount the changes, change the moods, imprison the sequences in a different order only to release them all again. And there's so much that my sleep is overwhelmed by the night sky, clear and country-sharp and moonless, so calm and dark that I cannot see anything except the Milky Way exploding above my head like an asylum.

Suddenly I startle.

A dull thud hits dead on the verandah.

I lie very quiet, helpless.

Fully awakened by their presence, I listen to the rich silence of two nocturnal possums playing carefully outside my window. Every night they come and every night they jolt me from my sleep. Five weeks I have lived in the bush but I am still not yet accustomed to its unexpected presence.

The possums freeze and look at me as I open the door. They try to stare me away, narrowing their claws which just grow bigger.

'We agreed,' they say. 'The verandah reverts back to the bush at night.'

18

'I know better,' I reply.

Slowly I am losing their night trust. Slowly they are being torn to pieces by dogs and feral cats. Slowly nature is changing. Slowly their fate is being sealed. Slowly they turn their heads and vanish into the scattered night-protected trees. Slowly I am left alone protected beneath an electric light. And soon it will be dawn.

Pacing the verandah I wait for the first rays of the sun. It is cold. The air is always cold here at night. No matter how hot the day, the stillness of the evening grows heavy with moisture and the wet crawls in to cover the apple trees with orange and green-white fungus. The climate is tubercular. Even when the snowdrops appear and the European pussy-willow bursts just before the native eucalypts and wattle (which migrants still choose to call mimosa), there is still a sense of rottenness brooding.

There is no spring here as other cultures know it. Only September, when the birch trees surge with sap and cover themselves with catkins, falling to make way for leaves. That's when my mother watches for her illegally grown memories to flower, grown from seed, scenting the air with a foreign nostalgia. The sweet smell of the past. Leningrad in May.

The local bush is dying. I know it. But I feel strangely insensitive at the thought. Still, I wonder about it. Like I wonder if the whole valley comes out every morning to smell the smell of new bread, that warm heavy romantic smell of yeast lapping around the morning mist and bird chatter. Reassuring, like the smell of your own piss on a campfire. Wombat Flats Bakery – a speck of light across the lake working into the dawn hours unaware that the wombats have all gone. (And it too is destined to close soon.)

Comfortable and blank, relaxed as one can only be after sitting up all night, munching on my thoughts, I think of Hass as we sat by the creek only the other day, maybe ten years ago. Holding bottles of freshly-pumped mineral water, listening to forgotten frogs courting.

We sat with the frogs for an hour. Hass holding a bird's nest in his hand. I feel close to Hass but I dare not say so. Our relationship is built on this sort of caution. So instead I say, 'I don't want to stay here any longer. I want to move to Sydney now. I don't like all this waiting around, hanging about here in the country, halfway between nowhere.' I say this more hesitantly than it appears written.

'Don't be silly', he says. 'We decided before we left Melbourne. It'll be easier if you come to Sydney when I'm back.'

Hass gets up and brushes the dirt off his corduroy trousers. He collects Art. I look at him with a quiet look that does nothing more than observe. I have noticed before that there is something strong in his consistency. His decisions mean to be final.

'But I don't want to wait,' I say.

Of us both, I am the one who is impatient. I am the one who changes his mind. I am the one who believes things too often, too quickly and too dramatically. Hass has trained himself to be more subtle.

He is cultivating a delicate love for the East. He will leave in two days time for Indonesia and Cambodia. In Bali he will search for bronzes and carved wooden deers. In Cheng Mai he will unearth heads of stone deities from antique dealers while I stay on here. It has been decided.

'Silly,' he says to me affectionately. But when he notices that I mean what I'm saying he turns his thoughts.

We walk to the house looking back at the man-made lake with its submerged Chinese Temple, gone now, made of wood, rotted.

For two more days we sleep together, touching and wrapping our legs around each other. We fuck reassuringly and slowly.

Then he leaves.

During the day in my wellingtons I wander the forest looking at mushrooms and lichens. I search for animal droppings to learn if there are any wombats close by. One evening, quite late, I see a platypus dive for safety in a part of the lake immediately below the house. The lake there is an overflow, smelly and dirty. The platypus will remain safe so long as the lake is not beautified.

I find a patch of coral fungus. Its colour ranges from cream to rich pink. It grows in tufts about the size of a hand. It branches just like sea coral and is delicious to eat. A nutty taste. There are no harmful varieties and it is quite common along the eastern coast of Australia. It is best fried with finely cut bacon and a spinkling of parsley.

At night I sit by the pine-cone fire worrying problems about relationships. Every night I have new theories. Some nights I sit up till dawn thinking about the death of love. And a simple problem has come to disturb me: I no longer desire to be human, but I don't quite know what that means.

Hass sends me letters from overseas. They tell of how hot he finds the weather and what he's buying. And of course he writes more, the things you are embarrassed to read out to other people: '... and I wish I could come all over you.' Ambarrukmo Palace Hotel, Jogjakarta, Indonesia.

While he buys ceramics, I collect mushrooms. While he buys folk culture, I collect pine cones and chop wood. I pick rosemary and cress, wander around the local graveyard and feel nothing. Climb the botanical gardens, smoke cigarettes and think about this man who seems to be my lover.

Later, I become aware that his purpose in going overseas is to collect the exquisite accomplishments of dead generations.

Later, I will accuse him of cultural imperialism when it slowly dawns on me that art treasures have become available from Cambodia because of the presence of the American Army there and in Vietnam. I will recognise the significance of corruption and international politics to the industry that supplies

21

decoration for the elegant rich.

Later, when I come to Sydney I will witness how the Director of the Australian National Gallery will buy a Mon-Dvaravati-style piece from Hass. Acquired through the generous assistance of dealers exploiting the American and Australian Imperialist slaughter in South-East Asia. Purchased with blood on our hands.

And Hass, with his love of refinement and his misguided certainty, is a pawn in all this.

And somehow it will affect us both.

And he closed his eyes on the effect on others.

And I gained a trembling knowledge into the politics of my own existence.

And something else showed me how different I was from what I would become.

And something happened to turn our relationship into a death mask.

But this is all additional. In Daylesford all I knew was that Hass and I had been lovers for six months and that we would meet in Sydney on Thursday when he returned.

HASS STORY

'Two days ago you told me I was being thrown over. Now you come here at midnight, and what for? You don't know yourself.'

Silence. It is true.

'It's time you sorted yourself out. You're not a child anymore. You're a grown man.'

Nothing to reply.

He sits back and puffs on a cigarette. As though clarifying some wisdom.

He has prepared himself for my visit and tries to appear

calm. Yet his foot is jerking.

His movements are studied as he runs his hand through his hair.

As he runs his hand down his neck and lets out a large long breath.

He almost says it's hot, but he's annoyed. So he won't relax. He won't participate.

He is there, six floors up in an apartment in Darling Point that has its doors closed every night and opened every morning. A private residence that determines how intimacies can be conducted. This is how some people manage to survive.

'Look, I know how you live, and I've got no objections. But my life is different.'

'It always was,' I almost say, but he sits up suddenly, straight, as though about to be photographed.

'I'm not saying there's anything wrong with your way of life, so don't tell me later that I did. There's nothing wrong. You come and go when you please, you're untidy, you stay up all night. And you have your politics. It's just that I can't live like that.' The monologue breaks for an instant.

'You've got to start doing things. You're in a real mess.'

'Thanks Hass.' But I don't say it. Instead I look away from him and stare at the antique screen (wayfarers on the wall, Eighteenth Century Japanese, five panels, signed.)

Hass puts his slippers on, gets up, adjusts his bathrobe and goes away to get a glass of water.

From the phone box to the flats, while I was walking there, I knew what I wanted to say. I knew why I was coming.

I was flying in like an unwanted mosquito to test his reaction. But instead of trust I found a figure who kept on repeating that whatever it was, it was gone. A voice that kept saying go away. I've found other interests.

'I've changed. It might have something to do with going abroad, but I know now I really like all my comforts.'

23

'Is that an explanation?'

'Look, you can call it bourgeois if you like. I don't care. I'll tell you something, though. Your radical friends, they like their comfort just as much even though they pretend not to.'

'Hass, I can't explain to you. We think so differently. Just think back to why we met and what was going on with you then, what you were thinking.'

'When was that?' he almost says.

'Come on! People don't forget so easily.'

'I have.' He looks away. I am not talking with Hass anymore. I am talking with his profile.

'You don't want to talk. You don't want to think or feel or anything. You just don't listen do you?'

'Because you're wrong.'

He says it swiftly. I am broken into in half sentence. My thoughts are jumbled by his environment. I am suffocated by the propriety of the interview. By the things that exist no more and so cannot be discussed.

'Sometimes you irritate me so much,' I say to myself. 'You know that when you're in a state like you're in now, that you're just tired. That's why you lose your sense of direction. And you make a drama out of everything.'

'Yes I know, I know,' I reply to myself dismissively.

The Khmer carving on the oak chest. Part of his collection. I glance at it. Quiet and calm, it has stood like that for centuries, not waiting for anything. Content to be made of stone.

Its eyes are closed to everything happening around it. If I walked up to it and gently lifted the eyelids, it still would not look out. Some things have been fixed for far too long, some-where inside, whirling and peaceful and final. Delicate, a head of stone that is out of this world.

Why in the hell did I think I could come to you anyway? Because we've slept together and fucked and shared each other's mouths? Is that why I thought I could pour out my soul

and all my misgivings, and that you'd listen? Why did I think
I knew you anyway?

I point this at all the polished artefacts carefully assembled
around the room, to try to frighten them out of their petrified
sensibilities. His taste. I want to encourage them to rebel, but
they don't. The Swangkolok pottery, the Mon deities, the
heads and torsos in the Dvaravati style and the white stucco
arm of a smashed Buddha, provenance unknown. Worm-eaten
and old, decayed, broken, dry-rotten and all wrong.

They should smell of time but they don't. They've been
fumigated and deodorised to make them last through time, for
ever.

And you Hass, you don't form relationships. You procure
attachments to protect you from some indefinable future. You
greatly miss the safety of a family, don't you. All those aunts
in Germany.

But no, there's more than that. You want to be a papa and a
mama come to visit the children. To get a kiss on the cheek, a
curtsey and the recitation of a few poetic pieces. Then send the
kiddies back to their governess while you return home to plan
the comforts of a tender old age.

Do you really think anyone will visit you on your balcony
when you're seventy-five, smoking the cigarette you've been
trying to give up for the last fifty years? And I'll bring you
oranges and melons, grapes and mandarins, but only unblem-
ished ones because I know that's how you like them. And
you'll smile with a twinkle and say to me, 'Oh you! You're
impossible.'

It doesn't work like that anymore, Hass. It just doesn't.
Things aren't as careful as that anymore.

He must have heard my thinking because he comes back
into the room. He wants me to go.

Looking at the birds in the persian carpet on the floor, cigarette in my hand, I begin to fold myself up tighter than I was
before I came.

'I want to go to bed,' he says. Then he picks the ashtray off the floor.

'I'll go in a minute.'

ANGER

Fucking is scum. It is a barren waste. Desolate. An arid wilderness. It is stagnation. Sterile dregs. Dross. Fucking is a wound. Worthless. A lesion I cannot heal. Sweating for nothing, my bedroom stinks of sperm. And lying in my sheets, masturbated off into for years, sex itself means nothing and leads nowhere. It's just another way of pulling yourself, this love which is such a disfigured enchantment.

Anger is not a good way to begin anything, let alone to end it. It is a hatred that forms like beads of sweat. I never thought our relationship would end. I'd forgotten to include our parting.

You became mine. You grew on me with my permission, a parasite, fingering, sucking, scratching around till you began to hurt me. I can't get out, I said quite softly. I can't peel away this skin. I hurt, my love. I am infested, stuck without the possibility of action and my mind beginning to charge around with murder. But I lust to keep on loving you.

(Some cold winter's day must have frozen my mind.)

When did I begin to see it was not working? Last night or last year? Six weeks ago when I thought I'd noticed you were different? Or when I started taking pills again so that I could sleep without the absurdity of dissecting a relationship?

I don't know when, but something happened when you began to look for other things and other people in earnest. Looking. That silent distraction, the hidden pathway that leads to fucking someone else.

Yes. It happened when we began to ask what we meant to each other.

(And the answer was somebody else.)

EPILOGUE

It is a long way home. Up the steps from Ocean Avenue and around Darling Point Road, deathly quiet at this time of night. A cool breeze blowing off Sydney harbour, the sea breeze of a night silence.

I flick a butt onto the pavement as I walk and watch it spark, turning into a chrysanthemum of fire for a moment. Lighting another cigarette, thinking on the extra couple of minutes with Hass, time growing shorter and shorter with each meeting, till this, our last.

I was there with him. I was trespassing. I was waiting for the final blow. And I walked out closing the door very softly behind me (as though I had never been there) while he was in the bathroom.

While I waited for the lift to come, I heard him lock the door. While I rode down the lift he closed his eyes against me. While I walked out to the street, his anxiety diminished and he fell comfortably away from ever knowing me again.

I walk. And while he begins to change his past to suit himself, a delirium begins to smother my head.

I feel too far to cry and I'm too distant to go home.

I want to watch the lights in Neutral Bay sparkle across the water and the wind blow from the Pacific through the trees and feel it brush cool across my forehead.

I'm hot.

My lungs ache.

This has all happened before, but in another sequence.

By tomorrow I will be feverish and unfeeling.

27

A funny reality begins to take hold of you when you first recognise that you are coming down with illness. It is a silent reality that notices small movements. It is like waiting.

It is a timelessness while you make readjustments. It is an eternity in which you make decisions about survival. It is a crisis in your continuity. It is not living.

It is true, I have overstretched myself again. It is also true that I will not go to sleep on my heart side, that I smoke too much, that sometimes I am lonely. It is also true that I want to be liked.

It is true that when I was a child I would repeat the word *nothing* in sequences of threes and nines before I went to sleep. I would do this in rhythms to keep away the spot above my head that would drip poison into my ear while I was asleep and careless. For seven years I covered my head at night.

I would eat bread with a knife and fork to protect me from germs.

I would not look out of the windows at night for fear of giant faces.

I would not switch on lights for fear of electrocution. And I was scared of the dark.

The garden at night would people itself with strangers, each one ready to overpower me at each unguarded moment.

I understood things when I was twelve that I have forgotten now.

Life goes on on two levels. One is the level of accommodation. It is this level that I learn about when I get sick, and each time it takes longer to become well again.

The second is the level on which we stretch, like a cat in front of a fire, like chewing gum. I knew about this level much better when I was twelve. When I could climb a fig tree and sail on its branches. When I could sit on the roof and wonder. When no one else concerned me.

Childhood is a heavy time. It thrusts behaviour onto you in hysterical patterns.

And then something happens.

Not when you discover sex, that's easy, relatively.

No.

Something happens when you discover that sex involves other people.

At twelve my feelings and my life began to confuse themselves. Patterns started to force themselves into me from outside my experience.

Like unwanted hair.

I began to avoid communal showers. I stopped undressing in front of others. I stopped playing sport. I stopped relaxing. I couldn't piss unless I was alone.

I began to be frightened of men because none of them wanted to be like me.

None of them wanted to feel me.

I wanted to be taught things no one seemed to know.

My fantasy at thirteen was to make friends, the sort of friends that know your anxieties and make allowances for them. I wanted to belong, to feel warm and gentle and protected. I wanted to learn about the ways I could be with men, but to learn it in the safe way that I was taught geography.

I would lie in my bed at night with a stiff in my head that was as tall as my forehead and firm as my legs. And it would rise out of my bedroom with closed doors into a secluded cubicle of a toilet. A night time toilet, with a solitary light, my trousers bursting with a fever, with a door with no lock, with the toilet being engulfed with the night shining of a man walking purposely in for reasons I know not why.

He coughs and I know he is there. I talk to him through the partition.

'Mister?' It is the voice of a child who is scared because he is. It is a voice that has been pumped up from somewhere deep inside.

'Mister?'

29

'Wait.' The process has begun. He comes to the door and says, 'What's the matter?' My flesh is trembling.

There is a pause while I make him say, 'Can I come in?'

'No.' But he has seen me for long enough to know what he will do.

'So what's the matter?'

'I'm scared.' It reads wrong but it is accurate. My body and my feelings need teaching.

'What do you want?'

'Nothing.' It is a lie we both know about.

'I can't help you unless you let me in.'

He opens the door while I say no again, but it is all happening because there is nothing to stop anymore, and he is in with me and he closes the door.

My clothes are on, but my cock is standing out of my trousers, rising and rising. An instinct tells me to undress. Looking at him, I am naked. He looks at my cock through my eyes while I grow up towards him and fatten out so much that I have to say, 'Don't touch me. Please mister, don't.' There is a longing in the way I say this.

So he crouches down and comes as close as he can without touching me. I can feel his breathing on my balls as the tip of my cock beats in tune with my heartbeat.

'Let me put you in my mouth.'

'No.'

So he begins my education. He tells me what is obvious, that I have to repeat my beginning.

'You are a man, and all men have cocks that go stiff. And it feels good. And it feels more when another man touches you.' He looks into me while his hand travels down, close but not touching. The hair on my skin follows his search.

Accidentally he brushes against my balls then holds them tightly so much that something squirts inside me.

I begin to breathe into my back. I spread my legs apart. I allow him.

'Can I feel you too?'

'Can I put you in my mouth and suck you?'

'No.' It is a fearful reply. 'But you can feel me for a minute.'

He moves his hand along from my balls till he holds all of me that is outside.

A feeling scratches down my legs while I finger through his trousers finding the stiff part of him I want. While his other hand begins to touch my bum and his finger traces around the muscle opening of my arse, I begin to unzip him.

'No,' he says. 'Not unless you let me suck you.'

It is important that he pretend he is doing all this for me only. It is important that I learn only later that he wants something too.

'Men really like doing this to each other.' This is the second part of my education. My stomach collapses into me and my shoulders contract as he moves the skin back along my prick.

'Okay, you can undo me.'

And as I reach into his clothes to uncover my first feel of the hardness that should be gently inside me, I slide into his lips and throat.

'No,' I say again. 'No.' He responds and lets me alone but continues my learning.

'I can do what other men do to each other. It helps.' He opens the door to expose me. I am more naked than anyone has ever been.

I try to say I want to hold him with my tongue, but he moves around me and moves his finger inside me, reaching into my arse. I am no longer in control of my speaking as he thrusts around, over and into and out, down there behind me, a thousand miles inside.

'Is that okay?'

And his finger turns into his body. He pushes up through me turning my legs outward, exposing my cock now beating in tune with his cock moving inside me fucking me. The world should be here watching what is being done, to see how I stand

31

as he spurts himself out, contracting.

And I walk out of there flowing, my underpants wet with a man, my arse penetrated, the wind outside blowing cool and dark and nobody but me knowing how full I have been made by a stranger.

WHITE NOISE

November 1960

Never had it so good
Till it all was over
Smoked a rotten cigarette
Chewed a leaf of clover
Everybody saw me grow
No one saw me growing
Everybody thought it strange
Till it all was over.

THE EXAMINATION

'Next,' she yelled without looking up.

A kid got up clutching a blue form in his hand. A lock of brown hair slipped down and fell over his forehead. He quickly tossed it back and walked to the desk. His shoes creaked all the way.

The signs of growing up were beginning to appear on him. He'd shot up quickly in the last three months, and his arms were long and gangly, quite out of proportion. The childish puppy fat had almost disappeared in his face, but the awkwardness was still there. It was only dawdling away. Below his shorts, his knees were covered in scratches and an old bruise.

When he reached the desk, he handed the form to the medical sister, a young woman of twenty-three dressed in a long ill-fitting white coat which she wore unbuttoned over her normal clothes. She turned his form over and marked something off in red pencil. Somewhere, down the school corridor, a class monotonously recited poetry. Except for this murmur the school was silent, as if the annual visit by the doctor had numbed all the students like an anaesthetic.

'Name?' she asked, again without looking up.

'Timothy Maurice Donaldson,' he replied. (Maurice was such a stupid name. It was me dad's brother's name who got killed in the war. He was a pilot.)

'Date of birth?'

'16 September 1947.'

'Age?'

'Just turned thirteen.' (Got a watch for me birthday. Wanted a bike. But me mum won't let me have a bike. Says it's too dangerous. She says she read in the papers about this kid who got killed, he was my age, cos the bus driver didn't see him and ran him over.)

The sister sat silently as she skipped over the address, diseases, next of kin.

'Ever been to hospital?'

'Only to get me tonsils out.'

There didn't seem to be much point in asking all those questions again. His mum had filled it all out at home and his dad had signed it. And they didn't ask anything serious like do you pull yourself off or do you know how babies are made. There was something silly about the doctors coming to school anyway. Unless it was for injections.

She handed the blue form back to him and told him to go to room twenty-five and undress, but to leave his underpants on and wait for the doctor. Tim knew all that anyway cos she'd said that to everyone else. Then she yelled, 'Next.'

'Are they gunna give injections?' asked Tim. 'I don't expect so,' she replied and looked at him. She had big black eyelashes which was why she probably didn't look up much.

Jakka got up and walked over to the desk as he was next. It was going to be interesting to see what would happen to Jakka thought Tim as he walked away. He never wore any underdaks.

In room twenty-five there were five boys from form 3B sitting on a long wooden bench, naked except for socks and underpants. Some of the kids were shivering a bit because they were cold or scared or embarrassed. Probably all three.

Tim took off his shoes and decided, like everyone else, to keep his socks on. He took off his grey school jumper and pulled the blue shirt out of his trousers, carefully slipped off the blue and maroon striped tie and lay it down on a chair, the knot still intact. As he unbuttoned his shirt, Hock, who sat behind him in class, came out and an old man in a white coat said, who's next? and another guy disappeared behind the closed door.

'What'd he do?' inquired Tim as he slipped his shirt and singlet off in one go.

'Nothing much.' Hock pulled his trousers on while the other kids listened to another version of the same old story. Hockney had been wearing long trousers for a whole year. He was every guy's excuse for getting rid of shorts.

'He asked me a few questions.' Tim rolled his long socks down as he took his shorts off. 'Told me to say aah and touch me toes. Then he grabbed me balls. They can tell if you've been playing with it. They check to see if they're sore.' Hock knew about a lot of things others didn't. Everyone in the room made a mental note not to react when they grabbed your pills, even if it did hurt.

'Did he give you an injection?'

'Nah.' He swept the anxiety away as if it were a fly.

Tim went and sat at the end of the queue. Everyone moved up one place. Jakka came in, looked around, left his trousers on and sat down.

'Gotta pull your pants down, princess.'

'Shut up, Adams. You got shit for brains,' retorted Jakka, automatically. Peter shut his mouth. It was hard to be smart

37

when you had practically nothing on.

Everyone moved up again. Soon Tim would be second, then he would be first, then the door opened and it was his turn.

Room twenty-five was the smallest room in the school. It was a bit of a mystery for the younger kids. The room was used by final year students for private study, and occasionally for odd things like teachers' meetings. It was also the inspector's office. The walls were painted education department gloss green up to about shoulder height. The rest was cream. On one side was a door which led into a makeshift sick bay. It was in this room that the doctor held court.

Tim entered and stood facing the window. On the desk were an assortment of instruments and a pile of blue forms. The doctor washed his hands and dried them on a coarse striped towel. He took Tim's form and started chattering to him as if he was an illustration in a picture book.

'Well, Timothy. We're going to do a few simple tests to make sure you grow into a strong healthy young man. When did you last see a doctor?'

'At the start of the year.'

'And what was wrong?'

'Flu.'

'Well that sounds quite normal. Let's have a look at your throat.'

Tim swallowed and prepared himself to say aah. The doctor put a silver object down his mouth, pushed his tongue and with the other hand shone a light down his throat. The doctor's hands were thick and white, the fingers pointed. Soft and gentle and sure in their touch, they registered icy cold when they came into contact with Tim's skin. There were tufts of light-coloured hair covering them. And they smelled of soap.

Tim shuddered involuntarily as the stethoscope plunged on his back.

'Bit cold is it? Not to worry. It'll warm up in a moment. Just

38

breathe deep. Come on, big deep breath. And another. Now cough. Nice big cough. That's right. And again.' He let the stethoscope fall and took it out of his ears. Practised fingers began to give short shallow taps across his back and down the sides of his lungs. The doctor's fingers now felt quite familiar. Tim relaxed a little.

'Bend over and touch your toes.' Tim obeyed.

'We do that to make sure your spine is growing nice and straight. Now go and stand over by the chair there.' Tim read from the wall chart, first with one eye, then with the other. Then the doctor sat down on a swivel chair in front of him, his hands level with Tim's thighs. Tim braced himself so as not to appear too nervous. His arms felt stupid, hanging uselessly by his side.

'What do you want to do when you grow up? Just breathe normally. Tell me if it hurts.' The doctor's full hand pressed deeply into Tim's stomach.

'I don't know.' Tim let out a little sound like an exhaled breath.

'Did that hurt?'

'No, I'm ticklish.'

'Just bear with me. This won't take long. Do you have any hobbies?' Tim thought for a moment about his dick.

'I like painting.'

'That's nice. Do you want to be an artist when you grow up.' The doctor's hand slipped down inside his underpants, his fingers feeling the almost hairless smooth skin around his groin.

'What sort of pictures do you paint? Landscapes or animals? Just give me another little cough, that's right. And again.' The hand slipped round to the other side.

'I like drawing people's faces.'

The elastic of his underwear tightened around his back. With one hand the doctor slipped the front down and peered between his legs. The other hand casually brushed down the side of his prick. The fingers fanned out inside the pouch. His palms pressed slightly against his balls and then the fingers felt around for a moment, investigating the tight bunch. Then it was all over.

The doctor swivelled off the chair and slipped behind the desk. He wrote out some details on the back of the form.

'Is that all?' Tim's voice was timid.

'Yes. You can get dressed now.'

Tim stood for moment, then asked, 'Is everything okay?' There was a pause.

'I think so. You'll get a letter to take home. You can get dressed now.'

The examination was over.

NIGHT

His room was an attic that had always seemed unconnected to the rest of the house. Into it Tim would disappear for hours and sit on his bed looking out through the window at the sky and the house next door, the trees below him reaching out over the wooden fence and up over the eaves. On windy nights their branches would scratch and bang darkly against the terracotta tiles like flying horsemen. But, like a sponge, the room absorbed every adolescent fear and turned it into a daydream.

Tim had strong repctitive dreams at night. He could not remember when they had started. Ages ago, stories had begun to overcrowd him, had slipped into him like a wet guest. Tim had been masturbating regularly for a number of years: the beginnings of sex were also lost somewhere far back in time.

He would lie in bed softly waiting. Then the sheets would warm up to the tune of his body, every detail registering in silence. Then his imagination would absorb him and reassemble Tim some distance away.

Not only his cock, but all the edges of his body would begin to stand on end.

He would be awake, standing on the dark uncharted land of perpetual sensation. A small red-brick building hidden by protective cypress trees. The fine mist of rain dripping from the heavy branches. On a green night. He would enter there and unlock a secret door. Carefully it would close behind him, locking him in forever. A single bulb. He would descend the stairs afraid of his footsteps rebounding off the silence of the walls.

At the bottom of the staircase sat two men. They would be talking to each other in soft low voices and stop as Tim approached. One would look up. Tim would stand as if waiting for attention. Some small time would pass.

What happened next was done coolly and efficiently. One man would get up. A set of hands would unbutton his shirt.

From behind now, another set of hands would undo his trousers. Two men would unwrap his body till all parts of it were made accessible.

Inside, there would be desire in their actions. And speed.

It was all performed like a prelude. Tim would stand there with his eyes open, looking forward into the darkness.

There was no reaction required of him as the fingers unfastened every fragment. Opened him. Touched him. But not undressed. Then left him available.

CICADAS

Everywhere has a next door. Next door to the Donaldsons, at number twenty-nine, was a deserted house built to one side of an enormous block of land. Although unoccupied, the house and the garden were kept in a state of reasonable repair. The family who owned it (the father was a doctor) had moved to

41

America for a short stay. That was three years ago. There was some talk of the husband going to work at a famous clinic. In their absence, a gardener and a housekeeper had been employed to overlook the property once a month. So everything, on the surface at least, remained neat and clean. The house did not dilapidate and the garden managed to bloom with flowers appropriate to the season.

Tim remembered the family. He had been friends with their youngest son, Andy, and they had played in the garden often. The week before Andy left, he and Tim had become blood brothers. Tim had pricked his finger while Andy had picked a scab till he drew blood. Both boys agreed that the amount of blood did not matter.

Now that the neighbours had left, Tim had, of course, been forbidden to go next door. This place was none of his concern, his parents said. But the intrigue proved to be too strong. The grounds held too many enchantments and there was too much mystery for an explorer to ignore. Besides, blood brothers had special unwritten rights.

The house itself was majestic. Built in the ridiculous twenties, it held, for a child, the intrigue of a castle. It had turrets and balconies and, at the far end, clearly visible from any of the surrounding streets, a flag tower which soared into the sky like a searchlight.

But the house was always bolted and inaccessible. The foundations were so high that you could not see into most of the windows even if you climbed up, and the ones you could reach were barred and firmly shut. The fortress was impregnable. One summer, a bottom door was discovered left unlocked. But it only led to the foundations and a small crypt-like room where the garden tools were stored. A quick check revealed little treasure. But despite this, the house remained a sentinel to magic.

The garden was a different matter altogether. It was large and free and, best of all, you could lose yourself into it for hours. Conceived along classical lines, it was planned and carefully planted. There was a tight hedge running along the white picket fence that bordered the street. Although not high enough to give total protection, it shielded the garden from all but the most prying eyes. Parallel to this fence was a covered walkway from which, in early spring, hung masses of wisteria blossoms. In late summer it became a mess of birds gorging themselves on green wine grapes, as small and as sharp as acid drops. The space between the hedge and the pergola was filled with flower beds.

In the middle was a pond built in the form of a cross. The fountain in its centre had not played for years and the rain water that had collected was now putrid. Its surface was covered with a thick layer of green slime and the bubbles of gas that rose to the surface sat captured like stupid grins. In winter the cold would turn this viridian carpet to a rusty red.

But this was only the antechamber to the magnificent odorous tomb that lay beyond. Preserved there was a secret darkness.

Listen. It started at the walkway. Here you were alone, safe from any human sight. At the entrance you moved into a living tunnel. The cement path was cracked and brittle, littered with dead leaves and moss and the white splatter of encrusted bird shit. Here and there, large dung beetles ran iridescently in their hidden labour, and centipedes and wood lice shunned the light. By night, possums streaked around in the moonlight or just sat waiting while house cats prowled and moaned away their lust.

The centre was a maelstrom. An instantaneous burst of brilliant forbidden black light. The centre of the universe was here. It was here that the earth shook on its axis. You passed here from one light to the next, from one world to another, from childhood into death.

When you survived, you emerged into an alcove lit by the strange magnetic light of overhanging trees. In its centre, as if in a clearing, stood a form: two griffins supporting a slab topped with a brass naked statue of a male eros. And here, amid the tiny resurrection of romantic flowers – purple violets, blue forget-me-nots, sweet honeysuckle and ivory jasmine – here in this calm remarkably suburban landscape, the adult world shook in idle speculation and was deflowered.

Listen, I will tell you.

'Do you believe in ghosts?'

'I dunno.'

'When you're dead you must go somewhere.'

'Maybe you just get buried. Do you think we should have a penny under our tongues when we die? I'm going to have one. Just in case. Otherwise you'd never get across the river.'

'I reckon a penny wouldn't help Spence none.' Spencer Middleton drew a moustache on Jesus in religious instruction and got sent home with a note. And he answered the teacher back. If you only had a yellow and a blue chalk, he said, what colour should you make Jesus in the manger? So he made him green and said Our Saviour was sick and made throwing up noises, and everyone laughed and Spence was sent home again.

'Spence reckons he's done over a girl.'

'I don't reckon he did. It's just fibs. Spence is just a sprog.'

'A fucking twerp.'

The conversation stops for a moment. The speaking order is reversed.

'You ever knocked a girl off?'

'Nup. You?'

'Nup.'

There is an inflammation in their minds. The conversation melts away like a touch.

In the climbing heat a harsh buzz appears, softly at first, gaining momentum. The cicadas begin to breathe out their summer noise from the branches far above. The scattered buzz rises like a mirage and drowns out the twittering of sparrows.

Only the occasional crow can cry out above the shimmering noise.

'Do you want to smoke a ciggie?'

'Where'd you get em from?'

'Pinched some off me dad last night.'

A sudden scampering in the leafy branches above them erupts into a hell noise. A bird eats a cicada. The insect screams, the frenzy of conscious death. Its soft abdomen is being pecked out, juicy green from inside the penetrated armour. And the cicada's wings ablaze with motion, beating in hysterical fear, its instincts wide open. In a minute it is all over. The cicada drops to the ground like a dead weight, its body missing. Only the empty protection survives, blasphemously banging its transparent wings on the concrete. Its existence disintegrates like a plane in mid-flight. The inhabitants scream, then the sound is switched off. The moronic noise stops. Death slams in as the generators fail.

The two boys swallow smoke into their lungs and watch. Their bodies spark, ignite, then turn gentle in their incandescence. A slow evaporation settles. A far off heart begins to throb.

When you're dead, I wonder if you keep on breathing?'

'You can't when you're buried.'

'Maybe you can in your mind.'

'I don't think so. Your mind probably dies too.'

'Then how can you know what's going on? How you can know something without knowing?'

'Maybe you get something else.'

'Like what?'

'Like a spirit or something.'

'I thought spirits were unhappy people.'

'Maybe everyone's unhappy when they die.'

'I suppose.'

'Do you think you're happy?'

'Sometimes.'

45

'I suppose it doesn't matter.'

'Nup. Not really.'

Lying on the ground the cicada spumes, its wings shudder. The final victory is over. Its wings folded back along the remnants of a green past.

SKIN

He bit hard into his lip, then bit hard again. There was a ridge along the inside of his cheek and he bit the skin all the way along the ridge from the very back of his mouth, from as far as he could, right through to the top lip. A strand of skin hung down suspended by two ends. He played with this strand with his tongue till it stretched too far and broke. Then he bit the strand off completely. Spat it out. Looked at it, squeezed it. His flesh, but no longer joined to him. Pink and long, he put it back in his mouth and chewed on it between his front teeth. When it was all decimated and the pleasure gone, he swallowed and searched the original spot with his tongue again. There were little strands hanging ragged from the edge of the sore. These he chewed away at, helping his teeth by pushing his thumb against his cheek to remove every last fragment. Then he bit hard, dredging the sides of the wound till the skin came away in layers. Underneath, the exposed flesh tasted new and metallic. Soon his tongue detected a faint hint of taste. He spat. The saliva was tinged with blood. In the night the little ulcer he had fashioned would form a thin skin over its surface. In the morning, if you worked carefully at it with your tongue, you could remove the whole surface and stretch it softly onto your finger. Thin and transparent, it would stick to itself till all that remained would be the tiniest ball of cells. The skin in his mouth would turn shiny again. Over a week, the ulcer would decrease in size till it healed over and disappeared.

46

THE CAP

Out from nowhere a bicycle swerved the corner and turned into the lane. Quickly, a mysterious hand swiped the cap off Tim's head. The leaves of the acacia trees had time to rustle before Tim recognised who the kid was.

'You stupid poxy bastard,' he yelled after the receding figure, meaning every word. 'Whatdaya think ya doing? Just wait till I catch up with ya. I'll do you ya cunt.'

Tim broke into a trot but his bag hindered him, banging about his legs. The bicycling figure stopped just in hearing distance and leaned with one foot off his bike. On his index finger he twirled the stolen cap.

'Bit tired today are you Timson?' The figure remained stationary. 'You been going at it a bit too hard I reckon.'

Tim slowed down, then stopped. There was no way in the world he was going to catch Mick. So he changed his tactics.

'Listen. Give us me hat back, will ya? Go on.' He put his bag over his shoulder and started slowly to advance with his hand out. As an afterthought he added, 'Don't be stupid,' for good measure.

'If you want it you can come and get it.' Mick got ready to take off. 'But I bet you can't. You been floggin it too hard. I can tell by the way you're walking. Your legs are too far apart.'

Tim advanced further.

'I betcha you could see the stains, if ya could bear the smell.'

Tim walked till he reached close enough to make a stab at grabbing something. He struck out with two quick steps but Mick had anticipated this. In a flash he was on his bike and away. The bike weaved left then right, then righted itself with speed and some quick pedalling.

'I told you. You gotta come and get it.' Mick yelled back with no particular purpose.

Tim stood for a moment then began to walk. He thought about what he'd do to that son of a skunk when he got him, scratched his nose and absently ripped a bit of ivy off the paling fence. He did that every day.

'Don't do yaself an injury,' Tim shouted out of frustration. Then he heard a threatening sound.

'Shit,' he mumbled as he once again broke out into a trot. The ten to nine train chattered steadily in the railway cutting below the lane. He'd be late for school if he didn't get going. To get late to Monday morning assembly was like suicide.

Tim really began to hurry.

At Avoca Street, Mick was waiting for him, as Tim had sort of expected. Mick was standing there with a grin on his face as big as a snake, wearing Tim's hat perched inside out while his own was shoved into his back pocket. Mick was standing with both feet on the ground this time, holding the bike next to himself.

Tim stopped dead and looked. They both stared. Eventually Mick shoved his jaw out, crossed his eyes and grimaced like a gorilla.

'You'll get it. Right between the legs. I'll rip em off ya quicker than you can use em,' said Tim.

'I'm scared, bimbo. Real scared. Look, I'm shaking all over.' Mick wiggled his bum for effect.

Tim turned to leave.

'You forgot your hat, lover boy.'

'Stuff it.'

The six minutes to nine was coming the other way. Both boys heard it. Tim rushed off forgetting about the cap. He was sure going to be late anyway, so one more thing didn't make any difference. Mick, when Tim had vanished, rode off with two caps. On a bike, he'd make school just in time.

Tim ran down the lane and turned right at the pedestrian overpass. It was quicker that way, but not half as much fun. It was only for emergencies.

He raced across the footbridge at double speed, turned the corner and dashed down the road. The long sock on his left leg

48

edged its way down his ankle as he ran, long strides pulled along by the growing momentum of the slope. The school bag was growing more cumbersome at each step. Just before he reached the bottom of the hill he let go of it. The bag went sliding of its own accord down the asphalt, the stones and the grit gouging into the black plastic. (Why can't you take care of things, his mum was forever saying.)

Heart pounding, Tim stopped. He'd had it. Late. Images of authority crawled around his few remaining free minutes. Detention. Extra work. Abuse by Mr. Hall. 'You come here sonny,' he'd boom. 'Society's got a place for people like you. And where is that?'

'Don't know, sir.'

'Jail, boy. You're heading there sooner than you think. You know where you'll spend your days?'

'Jail, sir.'

'Cells, boy. Locked up.'

'Fuck you, sir.'

There was nothing to do but miss assembly and try to merge into the crowds as they dispersed for first period. It was a risk. And if he was caught? If you were late, the degree hardly mattered.

Tim retraced his steps, circled the bowling club and walked along the railway track past the point where he normally turned off. When he reached the road he paused, waited till it cleared of traffic, then dashed across. There was an everpresent fear of being seen, but despite this Tim walked purposely slowly, knowing that he had to waste at least twenty minutes. Through the gully where the magpies nested, and he was almost safe.

He reached the park behind the school. It was a protection of sorts. Tim paused for no reason at the large conifer that grew beside the wall of the electricity substation. That was where he had once discovered a used franger hanging from the branches leaking fresh sperm onto the grassless ground under the tree. Tim went to where he had seen the wet stain darken the earth, and with a negligent curiosity rubbed his foot around the ground till little bits of gravel disturbed the surface. There was no moisture there anymore, only a wet memory. He stood for a moment feeling a lack that he could not put a name to.

But for a human sound which made him turn around, Tim would have stood there longer. He could not see where the sound had come from or what the voice had said. Then it happened again.

'You want us all to fucking be caught do you?' A figure half appeared from behind the hedge.

'Are you a screwball or something. Get out of fucking sight.'

Tim instinctively obeyed and ducked for cover behind the hedge. Four boys were hidden there.

'You watch it or you'll get pummelled,' said one boy. 'You're going about it the right way.'

'Oh leave the kid alone.' This came from a guy sitting on the ground. 'He wasn't to know.'

'Shut up, Taylor,' said the first boy. He turned back to Tim. 'Just watch yourself, or else you'll get your balls twisted.'

'I told you to lay off, Steve.'

Steve backed down and moved to let Tim into the shelter of the hedge. Neither of the other two boys had any reaction. They continued to puff cigarettes.

Taylor got up off the ground, rubbed the dust off his bum and walked up to Tim.

'You smoke?'

'Yeah,' replied Tim.

'Want one?'

Taylor offered him a Marlboro and gave him his cigarette to light from.

Tim took a puff from his fag, took it into his lungs and unhurriedly blew it out. The smoke came out thin and blue. It registered on the others that he really was a smoker and not a smartarse. At least that's what Tim thought as he relaxed and let his body slouch like the others.

The boys continued to stand around in silence. They weren't lost in secret private thoughts. They just waited, as they had waited in their late childhood for adolescence. And now that they were there, they waited to become adults.

Tim looked up at Taylor but caught a glance from Steve. Innocently he turned his head away to pull on his ciggie.

The late morning air began to stretch out and lighten. Nothing continued to happen.

'You going to the baths after?' one of the silent ones inquired of the other.

'Fink so.'

'You got your togs?'

'Got em on underneaf.'

The questions lapsed. Steve threw his butt on the ground and spat in its direction. But the spit landed short. Taylor walked up along the hedge a few yards, unzipped his trousers and started to piss. The urine trickled and splashed onto the earth then disappeared as the dry ground absorbed it. Tim followed Taylor's movements without watching. He was glad of being allowed to be there, but he didn't know what it meant.

When Taylor had finished pissing, he listened for a second. Then, like a leader to his troop of brigands, he gave the order to move out. The others, taking an instant to straighten out, moved as if by some prearranged plan. Tim followed.

The move from the park to the school came almost naturally. They walked, then walked in, looking humble, distracted, a little bored. As they mingled with the other students, they parted as a group and went their separate ways. Tim followed a few steps behind Taylor who rounded the stairs and started to walk up. Tim continued down the corridor to his locker.

'See ya,' he ventured to Taylor.

'Yeah,' the other replied. He was two years older.

As Tim opened his locker, Mick came by and thrust a cap into his hand.

'Where you been? I thought you'd got it.'

'Nah,' said Tim. 'I was smoking in the park with some guys. From fifth form.' Tim allowed this to sink in.

'We got French, room seventeen,' said Mick, appeasingly.

Tim got his things together then closed the locker door. Mick waited till he'd locked it and put away the key.

'Come on,' said Mick.

HOP TO IT, HARRIGAN

Sports day meant one of three things. You either nicked off or you stayed, and if you stayed, chances were that you'd either be in or out.

It was baseball. Tim's team was in. This meant that most of his side was lounging around waiting to have a smack at the ball. Every missed ball, fault or out call, made your turn further and further away. Especially if you weren't a top player, which none of the boys were.

'Maybe we should've taken tennis this term again,' said Harrigan to no one in particular.

'We could've at least nicked off quicker. Masterton don't care much.' It was true. Masterton was the science teacher. After lunch his lips and tongue were stained the burgundy colour of a few too many drinks. All you had to do with Masterton was turn up, change into your tennis gear, get marked off the roll, change again and piss off.

But not with baseball.

The noise of a ball being slogged resounded around the playing field. The ball flew, hovered, turned into its descent and landed firmly into Jakka's cupped hands.

'Out!' Mr Connor yelled his decision resolutely and firmly. For him this was a moment of educational training, the reason why you played sport.

'Fuck,' said Jakka as the falling ball stung and numbed his hands. But he also felt good as he heard Connor announce, 'Change sides.'

It wasn't long before Harrigan and Tim, relegated as usual to the outer field, forgot about baseball and began to horse-play between themselves. A little mock battle which landed Harrigan a swipe over the ear so much so that he yelled, 'Shit Timson, that hurt.' Harrigan stood rubbing his ear as the sting turned hot.

'Sorry mate,' said Tim. 'All's fair in love and war. You want I should kiss it better?'

'Oh shut up.' Harrigan stood suffering by himself. Tim understood.

'Sorry mate. I didn't mean to.' They both stood forlorn.

The sudden thwack of a ball attracted their attention, but only for a moment. The ball went off in another direction.

'Strike two!' announced Mr Connor enthusiastically, though somewhat unpopularly. A few voices protested, questioning the call. But this was also part of their education.

Harrigan cared more about his ear than fair play. Tim approached him ready to allow a reciprocal gesture of pain, but Harrigan showed no sign of wanting revenge. So the two boys just stood together.

Then Harrigan elbowed Tim in the side. It wasn't a hard belt, but Tim was ready to pummel Harrigan back when he noticed that this was only a gesture for Tim to take a look behind him.

A bitch on heat was being pursued by three dogs yapping and barking, cornering her by running her down in circles at which time she would stand her ground, snarl and snap, then cower and look apprehensively around allowing first one dog, then another, to come close and sniff below her rigidly standing tail. She'd stop then snarl again as one of the dogs tried to mount her, then she bit at it so fiercely that it withdrew, went barking off, then stopped to lick its exposed pink prick.

Suddenly Harrigan elbowed Tim in the side again, harder this time. A ball whizzed over their heads and landed in the outfield. Tim stood for a moment till he saw Connor running towards them blowing his whistle, and Tim saw Harrigan charge off to retrieve the ball.

'Hop to it, Harrigan,' yelled the teacher, pausing for a moment to catch his breath while Harrigan heaved the ball back. Then he blew his whistle extra hard.

Tim just stood there.

Connor came trotting up. He'd noticed the dogs. 'Since you two guys can't keep you minds on the game, you're both responsible for taking the equipment back to school after sport.'

Tim kind of looked away.

'That includes you too, Donaldson.'

When all the other boys had left the oval, Tim and Harrigan collected the bats, base markers, pads, gloves and balls and packed them into a large canvas bag. At first they threw everything in.

'Come on!' Harrigan kept on insisting. But the lot didn't fit no matter how they pushed and shoved. So they emptied the contents and repacked the bag more carefully this time.

'It wasn't my fault,' Tim ventured.

By the time they'd returned the bag to the sports room most of the school had left. Harrigan changed quickly and left too. Tim took a little longer and was the last to leave.

As he walked away from the building he unexpectedly turned away from home and paused under the peppercorn tree where the juicy-green caterpillars fattened themselves into emperor gum moths.

He paused for a moment, then retraced his steps.

Back in the dressing sheds the late afternoon light gave the room a special aura. The austereness of the wooden benches and the empty walls softened in this golden gloom till he felt as if he could touch its emptiness. The dusty warm smell of evening was fuller, more familiar to him here in this enclosed womb. Some small proportion of this smell was his. Not much, but enough to make him feel comfortable and possessive, expansive almost. As if he owned a part of its history just by having taken off his clothes and changed there.

Tim lingered, loosely and off-guard. He could have lived there forever, moving in like a forgotten hermit.

'What are you doing here?' Tim reeled around and saw Connor.

'I thought I'd left something behind,' Tim said.

'Well hurry on, I've got to close up.'

Tim moved to go.

'Thanks for bringing the equipment back,' said the man.

'That's okay, sir,' said Tim, recognising the attempted equality of the remark.

WAKING UP

That night the men were with him. He came to them through the door and down the stairs. Then the light went out before he could ask.

Tim stood. The darkness around him whispered. From all corners words moved in to tempt him. In the lightless space his eyes started to play tricks. He saw shapes, momentary images that swam past, guided by the sound of the voices.

Then he saw them. Ten, maybe more. Shapes that made Tim turn in his sleep.

Lying in his bedroom he let out a sound. A night cry. But this sound was not heard in that other space where he stood, far-flung, enclosed and fearful.

'Don't go yet,' said one voice. This made the other voices stop. Tim trembled. Almost broke off, almost disappeared. But that was only momentary as he gave himself over to the yellow light.

Someone spat. He felt a cold shudder pass around his body as if the floor had opened and shut.

His door was closed.

'I'm here,' he said and moved away into the dark.

He was now just one of many. And there were more of them than he thought. So he let himself swim like the others, like the many whispering moving shapes twisting like tendrils around a common edge.

So he went over and became one of them, without choice, like a beginning. Harrigan was there, but he vanished too quickly. Tim wanted to stop him, to question him, but there was Mick now standing by him just a little to his side. Tim turned to Mick as a hand passed over his back. Tim seized up, capsized on the tow of his own panic. But Mick reassured him.

'Don't ask,' he said. 'Just follow someone. Then go with someone else. Don't follow me. Learn for yourself.' And with that Mick also vanished.

Tim yelled for him. 'Don't leave me. Come back, Mick. Please come back.' But the flow was underway. His growing body bounced, deserted him, then reappeared as someone else. Still Tim, but now bruised and broken, no longer a boy, but someone who would now sleep with a million others who resembled each other.

Tim stood with them. There was no legend to learn, there was no defeat. Just an expectation, a quickly gained belief in what was going on. He tried to move but the crowd pressed tight against him. And then the sheets caught him and held him to an uncomfortable edge, a side from which he could not unwind. An entangled sleep. With men and horses and an erection, and then an arching of the back as he ejaculated a hazy stain into the sheets, the time of boyhood burst by a bubble of relief.

And the yellow light struck him, tearing night off his face, puncturing his sleep, waking him from his night friendship.

Tim jumped from his bed. A screaming form ran from him. 'I'll tell mum if you do anything. She told me to get you up.'

His sister bounded from the room.

'Fuck off,' he said, wide awake.

A MOMENT

'I can't tell anyone what I've been thinking.' Lying on his bed, fully clothed, Tim feels silent, plausible, inert. The world is quiet. Only Tim is awake.

'I feel as if I was followed by someone, but I can't remember who it was or where.'

Tim throws one shoe off, then the other. He pulls the shirt off his back, unbuttoned, then falls back onto his bed.

'I drank a bottle of beer tonight and the room keeps moving,' says Tim, without straining to understand.

'There is something I have to tell someone.' Sleep almost corrodes this insight, but he finishes the thought. 'Only the right person will understand. Until then, when I find him and tell him, I must hide it.' The room spins faster.

'The secret is everything.'

WHITE NOISE

When he woke the next morning, Tim didn't tell anyone but he was scared. For five nights he'd perspired with fear, a fear that mounted him, a full clear fear that shone into his childhood eyes like moonlight in the garden. What had until then been a shaky premonition, thoughts that could be ignored, now caught and melted him.

The moon outside deceived him. It lit the ground, made shadows of blue shrubs, created trees with no edges. Far in the close distance, the smudge of dark holes appeared where there was no light, edges of nothing. They came as if from nowhere.

It was like summer, this bright night, with no movement but full of light that a blind person could imagine. It was a bold move to stand outside on a night like this.

Tim stood on the grey lawn on this fifth night not daring to move, trying to obliterate himself – the fence in the distance, the lilli-pilli tree whose berries were the same colour by night as they were by day, the palms, the fox-green hydrangeas, the stippled shadows of the loquat branches, themselves splattered with chunks of peeling white bark, gone forever, and the visible fruit of lemons glowing as if they were all mouldy.

Still he stood.

A slight wind rubbed him, then died away, then returned again, annoying the shrubs and twigs, making something fall, dying away again, coming back quicker this time, squirming some climbing plants, popping a long seed pod close by. A hot flaking wind, puffing at intervals.

Through it all he stood, watching for the hurricane.

There was nothing to imagine. There was nothing in this night to hold him spellbound. But it was not as if he was comfortable looking out, feeling the breezes on his face as the winds scattered the blue landscape and entered him. They were vultures, these gentle shivers of air. The winds were the secrets, hot carcasses of night-time wakefulness. They knew no caution, no wish to know what any of their experiences meant.

The footpath creaked beneath his feet as the night turned cooler. But only a little. Yet he stood, quietly unmoved.

As the night turned around.

As the shrubs vanished, the lemon fruit switched off. The grey lawn spread into darker grey and then to asphalt, then disappeared altogether till you could see nothing silhouetted. Then it too was gone, squirming, collapsed like the rest of the world under a shadow cast by the sky now. Then it rained.

At first in this darkness he could only smell the rain coming, intuitively, like blue-bells ripening underground. Then louder, like the sound of butterflies flapping their wings or the sound of mosquitoes dying. For an instant it sounded like children going to school in winter, their long unprotected legs suffering the cold. Then summer returned for a moment. Then the torrent came.

It washed away the garden, opened gaping holes in everything around him. Yet still he stood.

One by one the drops of rain moistened him, then wet him, then soaked his clothes, saturated him, then dissolved him.

The rain soaked him into the earth.

First he became a drop on a blade of grass, then a dribble running down its stalk till he made a puddle around its roots, sitting on the ground.

When he reached the ground he was exhausted, but there was nothing to fight. After falling to the ground he disappeared easily, was absorbed like butter, melted underground like a reflection and was gone.

Underneath, he stayed silent for a while, allowing the portions of himself to gather. When he was ready he lifted his hands up to the air. Above him it rained for ten noisy minutes, then rained itself out in an hour. In the morning he rose with a buzzing in his ears. He complained, of course, because everyone was inattentive.

'I don't want to whisper,' he said to himself. So he waited out the years of schooling, becoming more and more unruly, putting himself more frequently on the line.

When he was expelled it didn't matter – he'd learned to drive a car by then. It was mainly on wet nights that he'd disappear to drive the roads of the city, watching always for the experiences of the next sixty years to beckon him. By that stage it was too late to explain to anyone. Anyway, it didn't matter. To most of them it would just sound like white noise.

WRITING IT DOWN
1972–1975

ROYAL PARADE, MELBOURNE

There's a fog in Parkville. A thick disquietening fog that refuses to lift. In the heart of this city, borrowed from previous inhabitants, the straight avenues of beech trees mould their branches into silhouettes, splayed out in a last autumn leaflessness. Not really alone, the early morning lights switch off as the first tram of the day hurtles past like a lost persuasion.

There may be other activity somewhere, but on the surface everything is still. A ripple lights up some colour in the sky. The fog sits quiet like a dead dog. It won't be moved. Not till actual morning when it will be lifted and replaced by weather of equal senselessness, equal frustration.

This is not a city of summers. It pretends for two months, but this is a ruse. The century-blasting heat of January is only a series of overcast days punctuated by weeks of hot fog.

Whenever I go back there, I think of this place as a place of obsession, a heavy hand. Like an exaggerated Valium mood, like a slight hangover, like things in the past that were never meant to happen. Imagine fine chalk dust, two days of no sleep, perspiration, dirty underwear, the caked salt from a dried sea swim – it is into this city that you wake to take an early morning bath.

Alone, you wrap a towel around yourself to hide your nakedness. It is not yet summer, so you feel uneasy about your body (thighs hidden under sheets, secrets in tins in desk drawers, awkward, like masturbating in the bush, in the dark, in sweaty shorts, into rubbish bins, on altars, among a crowd in an art gallery, a prison, over your father, guilty, like a monk).

Just before midday, the night fog begins to lift. You see it disappear in patches. Straining to hold on, it whispers through the tombstones of the cemetery opposite your house. You will watch the acres of graves in the Old Melbourne General Cemetery for a while. Standing by the window (as you often do), you try slowly to piece together the markers left for the departed, smoke a cigarette, feel immune from the fabric of superstition, drink a coffee and wait for the bath to fill so you too can stew the remainders of waking and last night's drinks.

Fully dressed in black, the first for today, a woman washes down a marble slab. This is where her husband lies. She lavishes as much affection on this memorial as she did on her husband while he was still living. Possibly more. She only resents him now for dying. He is six months rotting. Oh, how much dust has covered the tomb I have given you! She polishes the marble till it shines. She dusts off her devotion. But you don't care. None of her actions remind you of mortality. In the afternoon you climb through the missing railings to pick flowers: stink-weed, white love-in-a-mist, late-flowering piss-me-quick, tiny wild geraniums, a hollyhock, some shivery grass and a host of yellow and brown bush peas that will die at dusk. It is the scent that matters. The cemetery for you is ornamental.

You do not fit into the general pattern of things. You are a mass of extremes. This is consistent. You live in two rooms (bedroom and bathroom) while the rest of the house (four rooms) stand empty. (I will remind you later of the word solitude.)

The steam rises slowly as you turn the taps off. The weather is hot. Too hot for a day that will splash into sunlight after ten o'clock, too cold for when it will decay into another fog tonight.

You are twenty-four. A very late adolescence. Your character is built on residual tension, but age will change all that. In two years time you will notice your stomach muscles thicken into a premonition of middle age. You will be fascinated by these little excrescences. They won't concern you for another twelve years. You will look at older men then and you will re-read women writers with a new insight. Later, when travelling in Greece, you will return time and again to olive groves. And later still, when your eyesight starts to improve, you will quickly grow to love Pissarro.

The water and your body quickly assume one temperature and flow through each other. You immerse yourself, sink carefully. You lie like a cormorant on the tip of a wave, turn on your stomach, a corkscrew through the water, and descend into a submerged cave. Lying in springtime grass, the clear mineral feeling of springs, sulphur washing your eyes, mud bubbling over you. Stretching your arms, gracefully curving, brushing like flippers, wind in the wheat stalks, the smell of hay, the sound of a mother calling a dolphin out at sea – you open your eyes, inhale, close your life and dive –

Death is the natural extension of everything, the endpoint at which you are carried away. It is the finish. We cannot defeat that nothingness, not even by holding our breath. When we can go no further, that is when we cease. Death is the end of a certain kind of motion. Other things then take over.

Worms mainly. That is how things are. Slowly dying. Slowly killing ourselves. The negligent cough, a small pain, tiredness, nothing much, maybe a state of health, a premonition, a fog, it's all the same . . .

You splash up, catching your breath. Then you rest. You spend the next hour soaking yourself out of another uncomfortable morning.

Cutting the ice, the steam and the heat of the bath have removed you from wild forests, porpoises stranded on a beach curiously dying, the world gone wrong. Only, your head remains outside the level of the bath. It is always your head that protrudes out of the environment. That is your strongest possession. That and ambivalence.

LATE NIGHT LETTER

My dear you. Hi and all that.

I am writing you fleetingly after having seen you strangely for a moment. And probably it's all too foolish, but what the hell. So I hesitate to write, yet I feel like doing so. I've wanted to write for a couple of days. I sat down one afternoon and composed a partial letter. And oh how nice and gentle and wise I wished to appear. How much I wanted to set down words that would move you. Of course I ended up feeling sorry for myself. And then feeling stupid in the morning. Like a lost shark.

I wrote, 'I don't know whether I'm going to see you again, which makes it safe to write this letter to say some of the things I want to, and it's hard . . . ' Of course I never got past that line. Then I saw you again tonight.

You! This is a bit of a dither and a mumble. And there is a danger that I will lie back and write this out in my head, never to send it.

What am I saying? Superficial things. Like, I like you and I don't quite know why or how it came about. But I do. And then everything gets confused with sex and friendship and love and sleeping together. It's uncertainty. Yet there's the feeling of warmth somewhere in there.

You know, there are many feelings I can put words to. Like, I want to feel important to people. People I like. Flattered by their attention. Of course I hide this. Then there's the protective me who announces, 'I have survived, so I know how to be good for others.' You've seen through this. Everyone knows this strength and this kind of survival. Then there's the sex game. I protect myself here also when it comes too close, preferring the hidden comfort of my own fantasies with someone I don't care for at all. You know that too. And then there are all those things of friendship that seem to involve so many years of time, which is too long. Because I want to go through it all so instantly. I once wrote, 'I want lovers like a family. I want friends like I once had god.' I think that's still true, though I wonder if I understand what I meant.

You! Relationships are accidental. That I know. But I've been too hung up on these accidents.

Hey, it's late, and I have a heavy day tomorrow. And I feel as if I haven't said all that much. And then, I don't know what more there is to say. Except everything. Which may be nothing specific. Maybe just hi. Talking slower. Feeling more comfortable. Not pretending. Not being heavy either. Not demanding – something. I don't know. But there is also you. And I think about you. Which is saying what I want to say.

AGITPOETRY

Tonight I heard Phyllis Chesler who wrote *Women & Madness*. And Kate Jennings talking to her on the radio.

I found *Women & Madness* difficult to read, compounded as it was for me by passages like these –

Male homosexuality is often perceived, even through tears, as having a more 'glorious' tradition and a more legitimate or valued meaning than lesbianism. Historically, for example, many male homosexuals have waged 'heroic' wars together, have headed governments, churches, and industries, and created artistic and intellectual masterpieces. Some people think that male homosexuals are the keepers of western culture: in a sense, they are quite right – but my feeling about what this *means* is probably different from theirs.

and

With all due respect for the absolute and immediate guarantee of sexual freedom for all people, and with a respect doubly necessary because I am not a male homosexual, I must suggest that male homosexuality, in *patriarchal society*, is a basic and extreme expression of phallus worship, misogyny, and the colonization of certain female and/or 'feminine' functions.

A little over half the book and I stopped. I read no further of a book that ridiculed my living, that hated me so much for things attributed to me.

Kate, you asked the question that worried me deeply about the bits I've already quoted. And you said some men have reacted to this and when you'd put your question you said you agreed with the statements. By which I take it that you meant that you agreed with the general analysis of male homosexuality as presented in Chesler's book.

The reply you got was this (it is not verbatim) –

Most men in our society are homosexual. Men prefer the company of men. They fight wars *together*. They create art and culture together, and for themselves.

And then you read your poem. And the poem and the answer and the question may or may not have been accurate. I don't know. Because somewhere along the line I couldn't listen any longer. My feelings fought my senses, and my feelings won.

Do you know those situations? When you are so put down that the room around you tightens your perceptions and exaggerates your silences? Till your eyes focus on a distance that has nothing to do with anything that's going on? You feel so stupid that you can't speak, or react, or move, or look, or listen, or run away, which is what you'd do if there were no one in this world to see you do it. But you're stuck. Unanswerably stuck. That's what you made me feel tonight.

I wanted to ring you up after the programme. I wanted to ring and say, look, that was unfair. When you talked about homosexuals, you were talking about me too. Why didn't you acknowledge that I struggle? Or don't you know that I sit in my room-house disturbed for days on end like a Bach unaccompanied cello suite, not knowing the luxury of a social interaction or a past that offers me support, not knowing any bonding that leaves me comfortable?

Kate, you captured an experience about me but left me out.

And I wanted to show you my writings. All of them grown out of conflict and pain. All of them written out of desperation. All of them prunings of myself like the branches I've cut off the sick nectarine tree in the backyard. But I couldn't show you my work. Wouldn't. Because it's all unfinished. Because I get halfway through and then I stop. Because I've lost out against myself and turned distrustful.

So I didn't do anything. Because I had no achievements to show you.

Instead I write, 'Feminists can be poofter-bashers too.' And, 'I want to learn to stand against all definitions of what I and

70

my heritage are meant to be.' And, 'Kate Jennings is correct to agree with Phyllis Chesler's analysis of male homosexuality, but this analysis lacks feeling.'

Every time I fall in love with a guy, I perform a travesty on what is called a relationship.

VIRGINIA WOOLF
FOR BRIAN

Communication. An unalterable consciousness. Moods of death. Horse-drawn carts filled with straw and manure and heavy with moisture and sleep. Worms digging in the soil. Parsley germinating in the garden. Oxalis and sour-sob taking over the impressions I'd made. Dogs trampling the rest. I begin to write when I begin to take notes.

I write on scraps of paper, fragments jotted down hastily in the heat of a thought – on a railway station, in a room of illness, under a neon light, sitting in a bus for Leichhardt.

I start writing notes when I want to remember things, when I want to blot the knowledge of feeling from action, the setting aside of something absurd. When camellia flowers are insufficient for distraction. When cockroaches fall to certain death in boiling water because I push them in, you push me in, you drown me, you, the officer patrolling what I wish to be, become.

You stammer my sentences.

There is a deep black hole. You gave me a black hole inside me. Beside me, you stopped the first aeroplane of the morning from waking me from your bed. I began to write this in pieces when there was no more genuineness in the world.

I have become an oil rag floating on the ocean. You give me no more comfort. I worked in your garden once. I now grow plants in pots. You said you were sorry when I wept all night, tears of atrophy. Ho hum, I say in retrospect. My hair is too short to plait. And my interest in music remains unbearably verbal.

I use language to communicate. You use Wagner. I wanted to be a person. You wanted me to be an illustration in a dictionary. And then you hit upon the right expression – aposiopesis, sudden stop in speech for the sake of effect, *noun*. No matter. The phone has disconnected. And we were never parallel.

You had me as a vacation. I vacillated, not knowing. You worked to afford me. You supported me. You saw me as a three-day wonder, like the capitalists saw the Russian Revolution. But when you recognised I was a volunteer, you expected me to leave.

So you lied to keep me flaccid to your arms. You stole my meaning. You thought my writing was a pastime, a regression. You were amazed to find it mattered. But that is only now. Then, you never read what I wrote. Yet I ate your cooking.

Writing is a pointless exercise. Maybe. But it changes. One day you stripped me of my variation, and when I changed, you titled me mad. It is this that prompts me to write furious things, paragraphs which I try to keep intelligible.

'To write with the assurance of something you believe in is above life. To write with passion and love in the moment when sense and senses are collapsing, to write like this is to die in the moment of action. But this does not happen. Words have lost out. We neither live nor die when we write. Words have become consequences.'

My important actions were meaningless to your presence. You hardly knew they existed. Was it the same for you too? So I freaked out on consequences one night, one of those coolish nights, like three o'clock in the morning come early at a quarter-to-ten. Saturday night, car lights in the street. I felt more obvious than usual. Didn't know what to do with the night. Bought some take-away food, sausages and a headache spilling out finally what you were saying to me.

I must leave. I must split. Some responsibilities are necessary, but one must go on living. So I have to choose. Can I separate my identity? Can I throw out what I don't need? Will I be so tough that I can rid myself of the greed of being involved with someone?

Last night I thought of death till morning. Don't let it

frighten you, it is an intimate characteristic. You figured heavily till a bird smashed into my window. This stopped my thoughts. Is it only relevant if I love you as a protection? You are flying now, again, high and about. I want to fly too, but you hold my wings temporarily, for six months, till I rid myself of your black hole. But I am working on shortening the period. I am writing.

WITHDRAWAL

I am in seaweed caught. I am being carried by currents but I am not drowning. I am wearing some apparatus that lets me breathe in water. So I am continuing to live. But precariously. Without any feeling of control.

What is it? It comes in waves, deeper and deeper. They splash over your head the first time and you turn your head away. Then it happens again and you think – coincidence. You shrug your shoulders just as you are hit by another force. And then another. Then come the explosions around your thoughts. Sounds. Fast. Like fear. And you forget what you are. That you are a caterpillar suspended ten miles dangling on a slender silk.

There is no one listening. I hear it softly, in the shadows under the bark, in the little cracks behind the window where the spiders rest, waiting to weave their homes of capture. Small gestures of defiance. Happenings of life taking root. It is in the crabgrass surviving through the summer heatwave, waiting, in the leafmulch, patient. It is steeped into grey peppercorn trees, spring nights of hesitant rain – I hear it unfurling in patches everywhere.

Something that would give me no desire or dread, that's what I searched for. I worked on it, wore it for a day, called it my soliloquy. I worked hurriedly, fearing my mythology could crack at any moment. Something deep down told me this was insanity, a mahogany madness. But I ignored this voice. There was no time to waste.

What is this process called? Private thoughts, truth games, talking about experiences, things that have happened. Analysing, rehashing, distinguishing motives from actions, knowing yourself. Whatever it is called, it is bad company. I have spent too much of my time sleeping with it.

75

Two days ago I made some photography, small reproductions of memories and mists, of Daylesford and places closer to home. Brian holding an enormous mushroom. A birch tree that Hass and I had planted. Inez awakened from sleeping. Jenny and Jane laughing hilariously. Johnny sitting in a kitchen in Balmain. I developed pictures of myself too – images, likenesses, moods of reflection, crazy laughing pictures, awkward moments, social disguises, snaps of how other people captured me in a moment. I hid in my locked room at five o'clock in the morning to examine them, embarrassed to be discovered. Consecutively, and with each one, I peeled away my impression, removed the hair, the eyes, the hands, the clothes, the legs, the glasses. I removed my form. I peeled away my substance like sunburnt skin. Behind most of the pictures I found nothing but the white backing. But some, only a few, contained smudges, barely visible mists, soft mysterious activities, faint but actual echoes.

I am not sure from where it comes, but, first silently, a voice comes whispering around corners. A voice wraps itself around the sabot legs of the wooden table. It hides in the darkness of the sofa, spends moments suspended in the air before it swoops into another secluded space. It flows over my bed when I am asleep. It strays while I am reading. It is a harbinger of memories, an echo of images that twine into a buzz circling over my head till they collect themselves and alight on my shoulder to sit there with the full force of a presence. An echo with form.

'There is a lighthouse at the top of a cliff,' it says. 'Do you remember it? There is a rock that juts out of the sea. Its face is too jagged to climb. It would rip you, cut creases into your fine skin because it has no respect. It does not care that it can annihilate anyone foolish enough to climb the vistas of its peaks. You know the place. The waves come in there like the sound of a train passing behind clouds. You know this place exists because it was there you discovered fear. You found a monolith that could stop you.

'There is another place where you discovered the enchantment of terror. At first it is not a strange place. Seen from a distance with wheatfields surrounding it, you wonder why you bothered to view that small and insignificant cluster of pebbles. But then you approached closer. The flat countryside around you began to diminish in size. The darkness overtook you. You began to be held in the grips of some enormity. There were rocks suspended from nowhere. As you approached they transformed into immense fluted basalt spines. They stood with a width of something you had never imagined, their bases lightly touching the tips of a cavernous earth. Animals, it is said, would never go near.

'You stood before them for an hour. The time was too long. The sensation overtook you that there was a vibration, the other you suspended from your feet, hanging under the ground. It was your primeval shape. You did not want to see it. You did not want to know it was there. You fled, running through the bracken, stumbling, but kept yourself moving, careful only to stand where there was grass growing, for you were sure that there was ground there. You did not want to slip, fall and be swallowed up.

'Come with me. I will lead you into places that are secret. You will be warm and protected. I will take you to the mountains, into the forests humming with a light that is diffused and in such harmony that you will find the end of your search. You will reach the secret of the moment. You will hold it, balance out the weight of not belonging, forget about the grey-green moods. And then you will go one step further. You will become these things. Gold will run in your veins. Birds will lull you into a magic madness. You will become infinite.'

I dreamed of white crystal flowers and a festival. I was dressed like a lily standing beneath a nineteenth-century lampshade, opaque milk glass with violets painted on it. Then I dreamed of lying in clean sheets with red and pink geraniums growing on the windowsill, curving into and around the sun. I imagined myself there in that city, the sun streaming through the windows with the urgency of a summer morning. I was again alive. Outside, every shadow was stark and streamlined. As the day grew hotter there was a glimmer of walls slowly evaporating. Buildings revealed themselves for what they were. And behind, in front, around and in the walls, life was happening so quickly that it was too swift to capture in a second. When I awoke I felt as if I knew something.

TENDER WORDS

It is a slow process working into writing. There is a stillness about it. Words creep like gas out of a leak. It is like slow alcoholism – you need to be alone but with recordings of other people talking. Friends. Their talk thinking truths that are mine. Although my mind bends like a willow.

Maybe I am on the wrong wavelength. Maybe we are all afraid of exactly the same things, that we are identical, staying awake through the night smoking. I don't know. I want to run away behind closed doors, to Surfers Paradise, to Darwin, never Paris.

There are some boys playing with slingshots. I can see them from my window as I write. They are aiming at mischief. If I yell at them, they will hesitate, then disappear for a minute. Then they will come back.

Take the words from the page. Make a bed with them to lie on. After a while count the holes in each year that you have had a birthday.

Life has taught me to be cunning. It has taught me a beautiful safety. Talk to whomever you want as if they have become one shade lighter. Talk to them in your purest lanolin voice. Make them feel like a new plastic package. There is only so far that you can pretend.

I am not certain what I am saying any longer. It is getting too far removed. It will all happen, sometime. I live two lives.

Piaf is dead. I don't care. I hope she took love with her wherever it was she went, mon dieu.

I will know when it happens.

MICHAEL

No fear of the unknown, but totally paranoid when stoned. And whenever he's threatened, a complete resignation from the responsibilities of relationship and social interaction. An outcast, he distracts into himself and disturbs everyone around him.

'. . . and no ability to see through the reflected mirroring of many things in everything that goes on in living.'

But that is only one opinion.

I ask him, 'Are you afraid of what you don't know?'

'I get peculiar when I'm high.'

'What I'm really asking is, do you find me threatening?'

'No.' He pauses while the Mandrax further ages his beautiful body.

'The way you resign yourself from the responsibility of

relationships. The way you can close yourself off.' He looks at me.

'I look at you sometimes and you're looking at things that have nothing to do with me. I get concerned then.'

'Yes I do distract into myself.'

(. . . and no ability to see through the self-reflected mirroring of everything that goes on in living.)

'Why do you find you need to ask questions?' Michael asks me, off his head but very rational.

We walk to Hyde Park down along Oxford Street full of traffic and building construction. Congestion. Pools of illegal power resulting in an endless changing of the skyline. Somewhat aware of other people's needs and our own obligations, of the fact that time is moving, that we have promised to do other things, which means we will have to leave each other. Soon to leave. So I choose a dry spot and sit on the grass while he goes to throw some more pills down, slurping water from a park tap.

'I'll feel better in a minute,' he says. It's true, he becomes calmer.

We sit there on the grass looking up at each other occasionally. The park is used for pick-ups. Almost every park is. So many people living out their lives with others, yet averting these demands for a few seconds while they look for a new lover, find a casual friend, a two-night ally. And we, sitting on the dampness of the dirt, new-covered by a struggling growth, the grass shooting out from the rain last night or last year, an eternity moving around us, yet we are captured by this particular February.

'Stop looking at me like that.'

'Like what?'

'Like out of a cage in the zoo.'

My comments are careful. He's been hospitalised twice in a psychiatric bin.

'Have you decided yet whether I'm ferocious? I might bite

if you're not careful.'

We look at each other fondly. The sarcasm is immature.

'You don't bite.'

We are both high on drugs of devotion, but they just happen to be different drugs. So our talk is simply insane to anyone else. We are both of no interest to anyone, not to this city nor to the world. Only possibly to people like ourselves. And we aren't dangerous. Our minds are firm on that. We will sometimes glance into the general direction of each other, in case an interest is aroused. And then? We turn away and wander off into the direction we were going in. We carry no guns. We just walk on, to the car, the bus, the pub, the lover. Rare that, to be heading into the province of a lover. Rare. But not for lack of trying, and often we try too hard.

'What were we talking about?' he says, lolling on the grass. 'Was it about commitment?' The sun begins to shift into afternoon light. 'How can there be commitment after three hours? How can there ever be?' he adds, coolly.

So we talk about no commitment. How our feelings and wants are never specific, never the only real true things we want. And how we don't know what we want, only the general direction of our interests, which can be changed when the wind or will blows someone else into our circumference. When we are confronted by another set of indeterminates, another set of half-wishes half-aware half-true. Yet I know more than that about what I want.

I feel inside my bowels something wanting to be done in there. My cock rising again, but not too insistently yet. I glow. Do I want a fuck or a touch or just some more time. More time, more time please, mister. More time so that I can know what it is that Michael half-wants. I want to learn what direction he is leaning in so I can suggest it and intensify it if I too want that direction. A mutual want with purpose. And our talk continues through this imagination of the mind with the body rising and falling, reaching and lowering in its changes.

So we talk about changes. The changes that go and the changes that remain. Like friends we all have had.

I look at him in case he is offended.

'I've changed quite a lot in the last few years. I can say that I like you and it hasn't taken months of playing games with you to say so.'

'I like you too.'

He talks about more things but I can't remember specifically what. I've heard what I've wanted to hear, that he likes me. And so from there we can talk about more things.

Like changes and stability. The things that are happening around Sydney, where the Opera House has been changing into permanence for the last decade. The bungling that has made me aware of those years of growth in myself. The decay in my lungs by growing up smoking. The decay in my own reassurance of what time means.

And what if it should take ten years with this man here? What if we have to wait till we are both in our mid thirties dilemma? Or mid-forties? Can it wait that long? Can we keep marching on the spot till, years later, our directions eventually balance themselves out? When the Opera House is a fish shop, where will we both be?

'I'm probably the one who's afraid of uncertainty.'

'So why ask me that question?' he replies.

'Because of time.'

This conversation is becoming subtly intimidating. I'm stuck on a question I can't ask. Do you want to try a direction together? But how can I ask that at this point? The matter is one of commitment, and we seem only capable of doing without certainty. Without taking the bonds of engagement. Time is the essence. We want things different from all those promises we signed for and then found we couldn't get out of except by throwing things overboard. People packing their bags in the middle of the night and becoming someone else.

'Truthfully, how long do you think it'd take before we were

at each other's throats if we became lovers?' Michael is gentle but disarming. But this acts to force the realistic me to surface. The me that emerges when things begin to go differently. The man that says, be careful. Leave yourself an opening so that you can get out of these depths without the bends.

'So what's all this about?' I ask Michael. 'Is it just that we want to sleep together some more, or is there more?'

Pause.

'I think there's more,' I say and nod my head having said this.

'Yes,' he says and looks at me. His look is fully Mandraxed and is full of nothing more than sex.

We sit around and look at one another while the city intrudes into our penetration. If we were somewhere else, I think to myself, things would be different. And I light another cigarette and rub my arm and throw my head back and look up to the sky breathing in the humorous tragedy of our little talk. And Michael smirks, as careless with me as he is with his own life.

'You know I knew of you before we met.'

And I knew I was meeting you, the person I knew about. And I had imaginings of you. Your hair, growth of beard, the shape of your hands. All wrong.

Don't ever generalise, even on the specific. No conceptualisation is allowable. Never. We said something like that as we laughed, but not in those words. I have forgotten how we talked.

So what did I get to know in the half-minute-hour-three-hours? That I liked you? But I knew I would before we even met. Simple verification was all that first glance was about. And that we'd get off? The probability was there at good odds. Almost certain. Remember? I didn't have to explain what I meant. I just pointed to you and indicated you were feeling the same way too. Presumptuous, but accurate. That's the way I work. And you were feeling the come-I-want-to-put-my-arms-around-you feeling. You were, and you can't deny it. All you can say is you feel different now, if you wish.

So what else did we talk about?

Marguerite Duras and *Hiroshima Mon Amour*. Only because I was carrying a book of hers around. You hadn't seen the film and I didn't feel as if I remembered it well. But we talked about it because we were uncertain about anything else to talk about.

And I was all wrong about the story. But the actual plot didn't matter. The pictures were redundant. The story was more than present in the scars slashed into your arms. I wanted to talk about that. All the scar tissue reminding me of your suicide attempts. How many? One for each year of the building of the Opera House? But harder to forget than the plunders done on art. A scar is different. Special. Easier to construct but so much more contemplated. Sure, there are no mathematical formulae, no brilliant working out of stress and strain, of buckling and girders. There's no blueprint, no engineering. But there's a sense of time. The hours that you spend looking at your arm, feeling the veins under the skin, planning the incision, loving the razor's small sharp edge. You cut yourself as a matter of enjoyment.

It doesn't hurt. You told me it didn't. I thought it would hurt like all hell piercing in. But no. It doesn't, you said.

(It doesn't hurt because you hurt inside too much. Michael read this line and said I was a fuck-knuckle if that's what I thought. He said it wasn't true, so I cut it out of this final version.)

'You just cut the skin,' he said, 'carefully, and then the flesh, a nice clean cut, because there is no flow of blood at first. And then you wait and when the gush appears you paint the walls with it.'

'A deep act of meaning?' I fool myself that I can cope with this conversation.

'No,' he says. 'A creative act with red paint on a white surface. And there are lots of walls around.'

(I never told you that I couldn't handle this conversation. That the scars freaked me every time I felt them. Because they made me feel so much more than sex while you moved inside me, fucking me from behind with your arms locked around me. And I rubbed the scars on the inside of your arms maternally while you came inside me pained by the pleasure of your release.)

'Did you want to kill yourself?'

'Of course not. I just wanted to frighten people, and leave a mark.'

I try to make this into a joke.

'I can see it all. You lying there half conscious and everyone going crazy with the drama of it all. The red splodges on the walls and you opening one eye, slyly and cautiously, just before you pass out and are carried off, to check that you've scared them.'

'It's not as tolerant as that. No one is that understanding.' Michael laughs. He has left me behind.

That's why this talk has turned flippant. I'm trying hard to see for myself the humour in his gesture. It is a way of understanding something that's not my feeling. Yes, I find it strange to talk of suicide. It's not my reaction to vengeance or solitude or need. It's foreign. It's like meeting someone who's not really there.

The time Michael and I spent together contained many things not altogether to do with our relationship. We fucked, talked a lot and then he split. He ripped me off of about sixty dollars, took an ancient Greek coin and who knows what else. I minded at the time. And now? One night I went home and wrote a conversation with a dead man.

Q: What does it feel like to die?
A: Well it's sort of funny. This feeling takes you over, and

you don't want to stop it. I mean you actually have no desire to stop all the physical sensation that's going on because the sensation and the desire are one thing. Like an orgasm, except it's got nothing to do with pleasure. Pleasure is under some control. This is not.

You slide, I suppose would be the best way to describe it, or even that you're pulled along. And every ounce of yourself relaxes and begins to spiral round and round and away until you're all gone.

QUICK EXCHANGES

LIZ

'Don't believe anything, don't trust anyone. They'll all fuck you over. They'll mind-fuck you. They'll sit on you and rip into you. They'll get stuck into you and attack you when you show any sign, any sign at all that you want to be nice to them.'

She throws her hands away in a sign of, it's finished. It's all over, done for. I don't want any more, she's saying. Stop them, she's saying. I can't handle any more. She's saying, go away.

Her eyes are screwed up tight, closed in anger. But it's also that she won't look anymore at the world because as soon as she does it'll rip into her again.

'I just want to die.' She spits the words into herself to see how they feel.

'I just want to die. I just want to stop it all.'

There is a pause, then suddenly she's a different person who's opened her eyes. Someone I know again. (She's talking to me now instead of some fantastic audience of people she wants to hurt and kill and maim for the rest of her life.)

'They just ripped into me and I couldn't stop them. We were having a drink, and it was all pleasant, and we talked about the media, and then we talked about this and then we talked about that, and we all got drunk. That was okay.'

She looks up as if to say, that's the scenario – got it?

'And then all of a sudden they all started ripping into me. All of them, Rip, rip, rip. And I couldn't handle it. What sort of a trip were they on? They were ripping right into me and I couldn't do anything back. You can't rip into people you don't know. What did they think they were doing. What sort of mind-trip were they on? They were sitting there destroying me and I couldn't handle it anymore. I couldn't handle it. I couldn't handle it at all. I had to get up and just leave.'

Liz then turns on me, says that I've mind-fucked her too, says that I turned on her when she couldn't cope, and I knew she couldn't cope with the conversation. She says she hates me.

She then gets up and drives back to Newport. Before she leaves I ask her where she's going and if she's okay?

'Go away. Leave me alone.' She pisses me off.

As she walks up the path to her car she automatically stops halfway. She flings her head back.

'Elizabeth, pull yourself together. What do you think you're doing?'

She admonishes herself for being so wickedly human, then drives away.

INTIMACY

Paul went around to Judy's for lunch on Thursday. For a chat, Judy had said. For a change, Paul hadn't prepared himself for what he knew was going to happen. Instead he stopped off at the delicatessen. He arrived armed with offerings. If nothing else they would give him something to talk about.

As Judy went to let him in she again prepared her lines.

'I've brought some wine,' said Paul, handing her the bottle of claret at the door. 'And some pate and cheese.'

'Good,' said Judy. 'I've only got cold things anyway.'

Judy led Paul through into her sitting room. The room was dark and a little cramped, but very neat. Placed near the couch was a low table with a few snacks on it. Against one wall were two large bookshelves carefully crammed with books.

'It's a nice place,' ventured Paul.

'Yes,' replied Judy, a little too agreeably, 'I'll just go and open the wine,' and withdrew into the kitchen.

So as not to appear too nervous or awkward, Paul walked over to the bookshelves. He noticed a periodical and glanced at the cover. 'I see you've got the article on Roland Barthes.'

'Yes, it's . . .' She hesitated. 'I've borrowed it.' Judy suddenly felt hot. She extracted the cork. Thankfully it didn't pop.

Paul opened to the list of contents. There was Alan's signature, neat and compact, on the top right hand corner.

'Have you been following that debate?' Judy composed herself as she slowly rinsed and dried two glasses from the cupboard.

'Yes and no,' replied Paul as he replaced the periodical. 'Fucked if I know what a lot of it means.'

He caught Judy's smile as she came back from the kitchen. Judy didn't like swearing. But, as with a lot of things Judy didn't like, she didn't let on. She put the wine on the table for

Paul to pour, only because he'd brought it.

'Cheers,' said Paul. They even clinked glasses. Paul took a long sip. Judy just touched her glass to her lips, put the glass on the table and started to unwrap the cheese.

'Is this Italian?'

'I think so,' answered Paul. 'I like ambrosia.'

'It's nice,' she agreed, after breaking off a piece. 'Have some bread. I'll get a knife.'

'Don't bother,' he said as she got up. 'I'll just break it.' But Judy was already away. 'I have to get the butter.'

Judy came back from the kitchen with the butter and immediately began on her prepared speech.

'I know about you and Alan.'

Paul lost interest in the food. He nodded. True, he had expected Alan to tell Judy but it still came as a bit of a shock. He looked around for his cigarettes. As Paul lit up, Judy took a sip of wine.

'Is that what you wanted to talk about?'

Judy stopped still. She looked up.

'Sort of,' she replied then paused.

'Alan and I are engaged.' Suddenly neither of them was interested in eating.

'We were engaged on Saturday. Nobody knows yet except our families of course.' There was a pause during which a thought struck her.

'Not that you should be the first to know or anything . . .'

'I understand,' said Paul. He ashed his cigarette. Judy prevented herself from saying he smoked too much.

'Congratulations.' And then as if continuing a previous thought Paul added, 'This puts a different light on things.'

'It does,' agreed Judy.

Paul glanced over to the books.

'I didn't think that things between you had gone so far.' Paul got up and went to the window. It looked out onto a brick wall but he gazed there anyway. Judy helped herself to an olive.

'I suppose this leaves me out.'

The words were harsh. Judy let them go without reply.

After a moment Paul sat down again. He lit another cigarette. Immediately Judy felt anxious. It wasn't that she
doubted what she was doing. Her anxiety was caused by that
very human fear that she was being vicious, nasty – that she
was being a bitch. What bothered her was a sudden and unexpected sympathy, a feeling for Paul's predicament.

But then Paul wasn't dumb. He could be clever. He was easily capable of turning this situation to his own advantage. Was
that what he was doing now? She didn't know, couldn't tell
anymore. If only they could be more open – she would gladly
have done it. But that was impossible. Not with Paul. Not in
this situation. If Paul thought she was being a bitch it didn't
matter. That was the way it had to be.

Judy stood up and went into the kitchen again. 'I'll just finish making the salad,' she said, as she disappeared.

Paul continued to sit and smoke. When Judy returned with
the salad that neither of them would touch, Paul opened the
conversation.

'I didn't want it to be like this.'

'He's mine. He doesn't want you.' Judy was cold.

'How do you know?' The way Paul asked this made it seem
to Judy that the information was in some way open to doubt.

'He told me,' she replied, conscious of her victory.

'Okay. I won't push.' He said it but he couldn't believe it. The
pity he felt for himself was something Paul could not suppress.

'I hope you are both happy together. Genuinely.' He added
this last word to make what he said seem less incongruous.

'I believe you,' said Judy. She tried to make her voice sound
tender, but from that moment she knew she hated Paul,
loathed everything he stood for. But, as it is with such realis-
ations, it would only be later that she would express it in
words. To Alan in fact. She would call Paul dangerous and
wonder why either of them had ever bothered with him.

'I won't come around anymore. I'll avoid you both,' said Paul, in an attempt to make himself seem nicer. But Judy took him seriously.

'That's not necessary,' she said, avoiding the embarrassment.

'I've got to think of myself.'

'Sure,' said Judy, though she wasn't sure that Paul thought of anyone else.

Then Paul suddenly erupted.

'Oh, don't be so fucking nice. It's a game. It was always a game.' Paul tried to laugh. Judy, too, almost laughed as it became clear to her which one of them was the nastiest in this particular situation. But her relief was short-lived.

'You win.' Paul released this quickly. His sudden cruelty caught Judy off-guard but she wasn't thrown.

'And I'll keep him.' The reply was confident and clear. But Paul saw its weakness.

'I don't know that you will.' Immediately he said this, Paul regretted it.

'I will.' Judy made it sound as if her certainty was unshaken but added, 'He's chosen. He wants me, not you.'

Paul thought this over for a second. Then, catching a small glimpse of something else happening, said, 'You're fighting the wrong man.'

'Thanks,' she said.

Paul glanced at Judy in disbelief. 'You know what you've just said? What you've done is figured out another person's whole life. You think you're fighting me but you're not. Even if I could get him . . .'

'Which you can't.' She interrupted him.

'Can't you see. The fight was never with me. I stopped being in the running long before today.' Paul paused.

'I don't want him,' Paul lied. 'But you're not certain you've got him either. You'll never be sure. I'm not the man. You only have him on certain conditions . . .'

98

'Mine.' Judy said this in a way that closed all contact between them. Paul thought for a second then said the only thing he could. 'I can't argue with that. I don't know.'

They sat in silence for a while. Paul poured himself some more wine, drank it and refilled his glass. When you've lost you may as well make sure you've lost everything. 'Can I see him?'

'No,' she said, almost casually. 'He doesn't want to see you.'

Strange. Alan didn't want to see him yet it was Judy who said so. What was this thing that made people think they owned others. Paul felt it himself. But that didn't stop it from remaining a mystery.

'Do you want some coffee?' said Judy.

'No. I think I'd better go.'

As Paul walked home he thought, some people's fate is more sealed than others, then recognised that it applied to himself as well.

Judy, when she closed the door, went and washed up.

A MEETING

An Italian coffee shop in Darlinghurst was where I saw him again. At least I think it was him. I'm still not sure, though part of me is certain.

I wouldn't have taken much notice had I not been looking at haircuts, trying to get some idea of what to do with my own. And it was then I noticed him. And straight away I wasn't sure.

It'd been eight years. And then I didn't know him all that well. We'd slept together five, seven, maybe fewer times. Then I never saw him again. He was sixteen, seventeen, maybe. His father was a Sydney libertarian, so I'd possibly talked with his dad at the Newcastle Hotel.

I'd arrived at a party in Surry Hills. It was after the pubs had closed. We'd been drinking at the Cricketers Arms. I'd walked in and through the house to the kitchen at the back. He was sitting on a chair at the table, back to me. As I came in, he looked up and turned around. There were a couple of minutes as I glanced about, knowing he was looking at me. Then I looked at him, and he said, 'Hi.'

'Hello,' I said.

'How've you been?'

'Good.' I was trying to remember where I'd met him before.

'And how are you? I haven't seen you for ages.' His bottom lip jutted out just enough, and his eyes were merry with mischief.

'You don't know who I am because we've never met before,' he said in his low voice. He enjoyed saying that.

Later, on impulse, I walked over and kissed him.

'Do you want to come home?'

'Sure, why not.'

I try to get a closer look at him in the coffee shop. I am looking for some sign of recognition. That thing of not knowing, that you're not sure so you need something to reinforce the fact that you're correct. Then it becomes absolutely clear.

Nothing. He looks over a couple of times, but they're idle glances. He doesn't register me. But every time he looks over I become surer.

He hadn't fucked with men before he came home with me. He didn't tell me till later. I couldn't tell. He came around some more over about two or three months. He'd ring beforehand.

Then one day he came over – it was a weekday – and he was hesitant. Very reluctant about everything. Said he wouldn't stay long.

'Come upstairs and tell me,' I said.

We got into bed, kissed and cuddled. Then he started. It was so simple. He didn't want to be a poofter. He liked girls. It was nice with me. He really liked it. But he couldn't stay the night because he wanted to sleep with the woman he was beginning to see.

'Do you understand that? I came around because I wanted to tell you. And I knew you'd be waiting and that you'd be very disappointed if I didn't turn up. I'm sorry. Am I a heel?'

'Not at all. I'm a bit sorry, though.'

'I knew you would be.' He gives me a big cuddle. 'Do you want to fuck me?'

'Do you want me to?'

'Yes, I think so.'

He turns and lies on his stomach like he's done before. I put some KY on his arse and massage my thumb inside. And I stroke and feel him. His body is beautiful but inert. I feel for his cock which isn't hard at all. That's when he says, 'I don't want to come off, but you go ahead.'

That was the end of our last fuck.

I pulled him over and kissed him, kissed him like people kiss people who have just done something terribly unexpectedly dangerous get kissed after it's all over and thankfully they're still alive.

'Don't ever do that again.'

'No,' he says. 'It wouldn't have hurt though.'

And now here he is in Darlinghurst, drinking capuccinos and making intellectual talk with a College of the Arts design student. And he doesn't even notice me. It's probably not him anyway.

I pay – two caffe latte and one focaccia with cheese, salami and salad – and he stares straight at me, his bottom lip jutting out just enough, his memory switched to full-on. When I catch him looking a second time, this time surer, I know. But he's somewhere earlier, wrapped in my blankets, waiting for me to verify some memory. There is a moment as I pass him when it is still possible for one of us to reach out and say, 'It is you, isn't it?'

It was, but neither of us did it.

ATTACK

I've known him for just under two months. He's nice. I like him and we get on well together. We go out together a lot, sleep together. I think I understand him, and I'm getting quite involved.

He comes around one night to my new flat for dinner. We chatter on, drink, gossip. It's pleasant with him being there and me cooking. Relaxed. A new friend.

'I forgot to tell you,' he says casually. 'Our whole street was burgled on Saturday.'

'Oh yeah? What did you lose?'

'Nothing. I was at home that day. And this young chap came to the door asking if someone I'd never heard of lived there. Then I found out about the rest of the street. So I called the cops.'

'You what!' I drop my cooking.

'I called the cops,' he repeats.

'What for?' I am shocked into silence. Who is this man, I think to myself?

'But I told you the first time we met, that I'm middle class.'

He goes home that night because he feels isolated from me and anyway he's not having a good time. I spend three days worrying about my friend. I write him a long letter pointing out why one never calls the cops.

Then we have an argument about prisons.

I piss him off.

FUCK PIECE

I watched him emerge. He stood in front of my hands. My hands that have undressed him, pants down around his ankles like in a VD clinic. Ready to fuck.

Underpants are not functional pieces of clothing. They are part of your sex. Some men know this. You see them sometimes with open shirt and underwear clinging tightly stretched as they open the door to get the milk in the morning or put out the garbage at night. They know, the way they meet your eyes. And your balls go tight and move inwards and slide excitedly as you walk past, knowing those men aren't hiding anything from you.

Or in dressing-sheds. The man who combs his hair, naked, except for his shorts. It's part of the gear. They make you go stiff inside where it doesn't show.

Then he comes and stands close, to ask you where the toilets are. He's busting for a piss. No he doesn't. You are standing with your shirt open, underpants on. As he moves away you slip your shorts off. No you don't. You are waiting for him to turn back. He doesn't. He stands by the door of the toilet. You are to follow him in.

He is waiting to run his hand under your shirt.

You are waiting to squash yourself open against his open mouth, hollow with waiting.

He is waiting for you to run your face down his neck, down his chest, down to his hair.

You are waiting for him to tighten your skin back behind your prick. To make your cock glisten. To stop the blood from flowing for a minute.

Your cocks are strong. You have built them in times like this.

His nipples are erect. You stand apart, careful not to touch each other too closely, both hands on each others tits, sensitive, barely touching your breasts, holding your nipples between thumb and forefinger, jamming gently, just brushing past them lightly, letting them harden again, running a finger beneath and above, over them, pressing stiffer, squeezing, feeling the sexiness drain through and freeze out to all points of your existence.

Not touching, purposely, repeatedly, repeating, squeeze my nipples hard, harder, harder still, till your arse begins to open right up into your throat. Till you must be hurting him, but aren't. Because you know yourself how pain enlarges your body into a prick ten foot huge which is your abdomen turning outwards. The body slicing down the middle as you screw the nipples out of each other with your fingers or with your teeth now tearing out of each other some curling hair from his chest or from around his cock urgently sucking as if your life depended on it.

You blow him swallowing hard, knees trembling on the concrete floor.

I wanted to be torn apart as you came closer.

I wanted to let you get deeper inside.

I wanted you to open new crevices just as other men, not often slowly, opened me up then quickly held me open to unglue me further.

I had a need to be opened.

That's why I offered myself.

So you stand with your legs apart just looking at him. You are available and he knows it. He moves towards you and feels your cock then slips his finger into an arse, checking that you really want to take him. That your need now is great. So he spits on his cock and slides himself pushing in. The action is quick. The naturalness of it all makes you go passive and your arse opens fondly to take it all.

Take me. Take me with your pushing, sliding in with no resistance, a total accommodation of you, without a sound except the night and patient buggery.

S O   C O R R E C T

We drove up George Street slowly, as carefully as it takes to move through peak-hour traffic without stopping.

'Do you want to be dropped off somewhere?'

As I slam the car door I hear him say, 'See you.' If this was a novel I'd have myself say, 'It's too late for this sort of consideration.' Only, I understand wrong words. They're like eyes that never look upon hesitation. And the language which is personal experience vaporises senselessly. Like that! Click. Gone.

You drive away into a dream world which is yours. And I go into mine. I choose the correct expressions. You choose a better fantasy. But we both repeat, 'I do not want to be like other people,' in unison.

I held you in my arms when you were distressed. I wanted this gesture to say I care, truly I do, even though it's only for today. I fucked that gesture. I can see now that our situation was difficult, and that I wanted to justify my idea of politics. You were more correct. But I couldn't allow myself to be seen to be wrong.

That's why, when I felt vulnerable and lost and forgotten, I touched my head gently to your arm, a big sigh gesture. And you said to me, 'I think you're a bit pissed.'

'No, I'm not.' I said.

There was a sort of smile humming around us that day. But neither of us smiled.

Politics kill love. But we need both. That's why I wanted to hug you forever. That's also why you had to close off from me.

Someone has to start.

I can see now why I was shattered when, one week after I'd met you, you said you found me hollow. I didn't think I was.

How would you react if you were me?

ROMANCE

'What is love?' I asked Inez one day.

'Love only happens once in your life. Because if it happens more than once it's not True Love. That only happens once and it's happened to me. Unfortunately it was when I was thirteen and I fell in love with Christopher. I feel so sad sometimes that I've been in love and it was so long ago and I was so young. It can never happen again.

'I didn't know what it was then, so I thought it was good but nothing special. Now I know it was true love. Your first love is always your true love, did you know that? And it's also your last. So Christopher will always stay special for me. Sometimes I wish I'd waited but you never can. It's all accidental. Otherwise I really wouldn't even think of him or probably even like him. If I met him now I'd hate him. But I don't, because he's my One True Love and the only I'll ever have. That's what love is.'

'But what did it feel like?'

'Oh, you know, different. I don't remember. I'll have to look it up in my diary.'

DIARY EXTRACT

'Dear diary. Today was nothing more than any of my days except that I thought about C. all day. Well mostly all day. You remember I told you how he kissed me and I didn't know what I should do? Well, I know now. Wrote a letter to my Canadian pen friend. Made three phone calls, one real long. Time to turn the lights off. Oh well! Another day.'

NEVER BLUE

'The only thing I regret is that I didn't persevere and become a good musician.' She says this without the slightest hint of nostalgia.

'It's true.' And with this fact established, she pours herself the last dregs from the just-warm teapot. Two sips.

They sit silently as friends do at the end of a lunch. Before the preparations for evening begin.

Her friend smokes away at her rolled tobacco. The late summer scent of warm smells drifts in through the open kitchen door.

'You know, in a funny way we've both been lucky.'

The used plates, the bowl with the remnants of a tossed salad sticking to its sides, the wine glasses and teacups, and the ashtray with dead matches, butts and olive pits carpet the table and grow around them.

'The way we're still able to talk the way we did then years ago.' And the silence slips back in, unthreatening, friendly.

'You know,' she hesitates. 'I never was all that good on the piano. I had potential. That was it. And a bit of style.' She looks out the window at nothing in particular. And then looks back at her friend.

'I wasn't bad though. I used to think then that I was stunning them. I used to pretend a lot and cheat at the difficult bits. Go loud and technical and whizz up and down the keys and then go pianissimo, really soft. It was really big deal.'

Another small moment. Then with the realism of clear reflection she suddenly says, 'Ambition has really avoided us. It's as if I miss something big and huge, an achievement of some sort. And at the same time I feel lucky that it's not there. That I've avoided it. I feel better for it.'

'And worse,' intervenes her friend. Both things are true for both of them.

'I've been spouting off too much,' she says, finally.

'No. Go on. It's not something you talk much about.'

And then another quietness. The self-absorption of memory. The reminiscence of discovering the past for someone else. A totally commonplace creative act.

'Go on, I want to listen to some more.' And she rolls some more tobacco, pulling out the bits poking out at both ends, fixing it till it is ready to be lit.

After it is alight, she says, 'Let's have a bit of brandy.'

'Good idea.'

The first gulp goes down swift and sure, mapping out its own route till it ends mellow and exact. Soft.

'The first sip is always the best.' The broad ramifications of this sensation do not go unnoticed.

'Funnily enough my mother always regretted not having any musical training. Your family was different. There was always music in the house. We never had any. None at all. I still don't understand her resentment. Maybe it had something to do with class. Something like if you could sing or go to concerts you were somehow better.' She puffs on her cigarette and swallows some more brandy.

'She drank gin and grew roses.'

Brushing away her hair she says, 'I really don't like roses. Sometimes I think I like the wild pink ones with five petals, the ones with clusters of tiny sharp thorns, the ones that get rose-hips in winter. Or the old-fashioned single white ones. Pure white, you know the ones I mean? We had this rose corner at the back of the yard. It was where the dead dogs got buried. And there was a white rose with a fantastic scent. It was always very tightly closed, compact they call it. And the buds, the outside petals would go yellow and shrivel up just before it would open.'

They pour another brandy.

'And at the other end near the lemon tree was a glorious vel-vet red. Drops of water would sit on the petals. Round fat globs of water, which if you touched them would run inside and leave no marks. No traces at all. She picked one of them when my father died. Early in the morning, a fully opened one. You know, one of those ones which will be too far gone by the next day. She spent a long time choosing it, but it was really only a couple of minutes. Then she held it all morning with a piece of grease-proof paper around it and put it into his coffin just before the lid went on. And the petals just all fell off.'

The brandy slips down easily now.

'Between the white rose and the red one were all these eight or ten plants, all these pale mauve, washed-out, not quite any-thing colour, really unattractive . . .'

The description of the colour makes her falter.

'She wanted to grow blue roses. Someone will breed one one day, she'd say, and they'll make a fortune. So she grew these pale approximations. Almost blue. Not quite blue. Possibly bluish. I don't know that that explains her fixation on music.'

Something very warm assisted by the brandy melts her

memory. A vase of green zinnias, a lunch present for her friend, stands uncritically on the sideboard in the room off the kitchen as they sip more brandy and sit.

———————

'I have to go to Melbourne.' Ruth's phone voice is sharp and cool.

'Is everything all right?'

'No. My mother's dying.' It is late afternoon.

'Can I drive you to the airport? Or anything?'

'No. There's a flight at five-fifteen. I'm waiting for the taxi.' She takes a puff of her cigarette.

'I think I'll be too late. Could you feed the Tom?'

'Sure.'

'I've left some cans out. Don't bother about the morning, just half a can at night. If he complains, give him a kick. I'll leave ten dollars, that should cover it. He likes a change sometimes from his Pilchards in Aspic.'

'Have you got enough money?'

'I'm going on a dud cheque, first class. I'll put the hard word on Harry when I get there. It'll be okay.'

'Are you all right?'

'I don't know. I'll ring you.'

'Please do.'

'I will. I've got to go now.'

'Ring me.'

'Sure. Don't go to any trouble with the Tom. He's missed a meal before.'

'Ring reverse charges.'

'Thanks. Don't go to any trouble. Bye.'

It took about a minute for the plane to turn, then it stopped. As the engine hushed, everything relaxed. The jet stood alone in a field of grass shining like an idol, pausing for that last moment before everything changed. Then it began.

Without warning, the vibrations of the engine started to increase, the noise waved about in patterns. Unseen movements gave life to the air, lifted it and circulated it through the turbines. Second by second the people inside were cut away from their surroundings. A cord stretched beyond breaking. The grip started to loosen, then snapped. In an instant everything began to move.

As the thrust of acceleration increased, Ruth's memory rushed forward. The noise jumbled everything that was left behind, threw her mind into a haphazard order, tipped everything up and scattered the pieces. For one moment everything stood horribly heavy. Then the pressure began. The back wheels cracked off the ground and everything that remained fell away. A new order returned.

The tarmac gave way to grass and the grass to paddocks crossed by roads and tracks. People merged into cars and the cars disappeared into small spots of moving colour on the winding curves of a freeway. Then the colours vanished and the buildings blurred. Everything was transformed into a distant topography of hard edges and numbers and names of streets in an old address book.

Then everything vanished into white. The no-smoking sign went off. Passengers began to unbuckle their seat-belts. The hostesses began their movements around the aisles. Ruth lit a cigarette and looked out.

The clouds were gathered thickly beneath her, shining in a dazzling reflection of the sun, three or four hours before sunset. The world had grown bigger and more spacious as she looked out of the double glass. Somewhere underneath they were casting a shadow. And somewhere further down, other things were happening. Small things, she thought, and then thought of her mother and her eyes clouded over.

Below, great edges of brown and red and newly-green agricultural expanses contrasted with the unknown dark irregular green slabs where wild forces still acted on the landscape, protecting it from human change. The rock-strewn hilltops, the scarps, the gashes of the gorges, the struggling streams and billabongs. And somewhere, distinctly distanced, little clusters of houses and strung-out towns where people were at that very moment shopping in supermarkets or digging in their gardens, attempting to stem the rough untidy growth of nature. It was true. They were small things when you weren't there.

But up here in the air everything was big. Nothing mattered in this suspension. Everything here happened on a grand scale. Life did not exist and survival was on too small a scale to matter. Death disappeared into endlessness, a perception only of leaving everything behind.

As she removed the cellophane from the biscuits, Ruth thought, it's silly to feel guilty. She tried to justify this to herself, but it wasn't necessary.

You always know. In the first moment of knowing something, you know everything. It is immediate and unexpected – quick knowledge, like a jetplane falling through an airpocket. Experience may be the true reflection of the subconscious. Maybe. Certainly the past is always human. But there was more to it than that.

Looking through the window, trying to discern the mark of the horizon far away, Ruth experienced suddenly, and for the first time, the knowledge that everyone grows older only in environments with total strangers.

North Fitzroy.

Helen my dear,

After ringing you up last week and not ringing from here

because I can't and not knowing why I couldn't lift the receiver and dial your number. The directness of it all was too much to bear. Keeping in touch is sometimes too difficult even when you want to do so passionately. That need to talk. I wish we were in your kitchen with a bottle of brandy instead of being stuck here with the family all closing rank around one another, not letting mortality and their own wickedness get the better of them.

The funeral was awful. *What is one meant to do?* I arrived and mum was dead. Poor mum. Thankfully she didn't suffer, just slipped into a coma and after a while just died.

The fights! First they all wanted a post-mortem. What the hell for? To find out she'd died of a broken heart? Or of too much living? I don't know why I fought, but I did. And finally I simply yelled – let her be! Leave her alone!

I felt like some shrill, hysterical female. I tried to act rationally. I didn't break down till it was well and truly over, though I felt, god did I feel. And then it wasn't only grief. It was anger. The tears of loss but the wailing of anger. Helen I hate them.

Everyone knew. Harry and Keith in particular, but everyone else did too. She wanted a cremation, and they organised a burial, with my father, together in one tomb, one on top of the other for eternity.

She didn't want that. She'd hardly wanted a funeral. Ages ago, when dad died she'd said, just chuck me out on a garbage dump. She didn't leave strict instructions but everyone knew she wanted to be burnt and her ashes thrown to the wind. Annette (remember her?) well she and I had a chat afterwards and she said, 'Come over to Keith's place for a wake. Forget the fight, this is no time for that sort of thing.' I thought for a moment she'd say what's done is done!

She's dead, and it's all so stupid. But it was her wish and her will and her body and her life. Her decision. You know all that stuff. And those fucking Men, my Brothers, making Her Decisions.

117

Was it just grief? Was that what my anger was? I don't know. But I don't think so.

I hate them for what they did. Their betrayal was cruel. I couldn't stand up to the lot of them. So I went to Keith's and I drank. They were polite. I was polite. I drank more. They got wistful, I got quietly resentful. They got remorseful, I got angry. And then everyone, kids and all, were called in for a final memorial reminiscence. And they all had their say. Then Harry, being the head of the family now in his own right said, 'Let's have a quiet minute for mum.'

The silence started. It wrangled my nerves. So with their heads bowed low I quietly said, 'This is not what she wanted. She would have hated this. At least she's on top of him.' And I left.

Helen, I've never done better, and I'm ashamed and sad. Missing you and the Tom.

Love,

ℛ.

ps. I feel so old.

'Nothing's like it should be,' she says. 'I suppose it's what used to be called a loss of innocence. Funny how I talked to you about her just before it happened. And here we are again sitting together drinking brandy. Right from the start this time.'

Lighting another cigarette, she brushes some ash off the table and lets out a heavy puff. 'It's all so unexpected. You're never really prepared. I know it's crap but it's like being in a dream. Ten o'clock in the morning and here we are drinking brandy and smoking cigarettes. I'm so relieved it's all over.'

'Thanks,' she says out of the blue. And then pursuing an earlier thought says, 'The natural order of things is fucked.'

She laughs. 'It is fucked. Totally.' And downs the brandy. 'I'm going to get really drunk if I don't watch it.'

A quietness wraps itself around both of them. Inner thoughts pass silently, release themselves and disappear.

'Do you mind if I take my shoes off?' This is not something she should have to ask. It is a question of being past grief.

'Oh, I am getting drunk. But it is nice being somewhere where you don't have to care. Beyond care!' She says this positively, then suddenly again, 'Thanks.'

They glance at each other. There is no need for a reply.

'I really pissed them off you know. Not with all that stuff I wrote you about. No, I got them where it hurt. All that emotional side that apparently didn't matter to them. It was funny, after the funeral, it was as if I'd gone to pieces. Which I had. And so it was me going all loony and them being so together, the organisers of the family. No support. Their feelings were somewhere else.'

Another cigarette, another brandy, she pours them.

'I hate them you know. So I went and cried by myself. I wrote you the letter. Then I went to bed. Of course I couldn't sleep. If I was here I'd get some pills, have a drink, bomb myself out for a day or two.'

She puffs a cigarette as if it's a delightful but frantic memory.

'I lay in bed and planned it. I planned everything. It was about five in the morning and I know this was totally loony, but at five I got up and went around to her house. It was quiet – you know what Melbourne suburbs are like – and I went around . . .' She takes some more brandy and laughs.

'I don't know why. I really don't. It was like an instinct. And I don't know where the thought came from, but I just went to the house and pruned the roses. All of them.'

'Did you do a good job?'

'Sure! Then I rang them all up. They were pretty pissed off at that time of the morning and I was pretty exhausted but I arranged it.'

119

Pause.

'They'd been through the house. Can you believe that? They'd gone right through! That was what annoyed me most. I don't know what they took and I don't care, but they'd been there. Imagine that. So what I did was went around and plugged up the bath, the wash-basins, the kitchen sink and the laundry tub, I filled them up with water and I went around all of them and pissed in them all. And when they turned up the next day I said to them, let's talk about the inheritance.'

The mood turns to hilarity, a secret shared between friends, broad laughter followed by a real disturbing silence.

'The place was left to the three of us, equally. So Carol said that she and Harry would eventually like to live there and since I lived in Sydney and had no children and Annette and Keith were set up . . . I said, okay, buy me out. And Harry said, I'll offer you what your share's worth, straight out sale. I said yes, see my lawyers. We shook on it. It took all of two minutes. Then Carol said, do you want to take anything? I said, yes, if there is anything left worth taking. And I'll stay here tonight if you don't mind. So I slept in my mother's bed. I took her kettle, the washing machine, a few photos and the vase for you.'

The old cut crystal vase, a wedding present, standing on the side-board with fuchsias in it.

'Then I went outside and pulled out the roses, every one of them.'

There is a long pause. Ruth smiles a half-tired, half-drunk, half-confused smile.

'It hasn't been easy,' she says.

'I suppose life falls into three phases. Childhood is the most forgettable.'

120

'Other people's rules.'

'I was totally taken in by the threat of what would happen if I didn't obey, so I was really good and thoughtful. If I met me now I'd hate me.' She emphasises the word hate. It's revenge of a kind.

'I was going to say that you can't expect the kind of rebellion we're used to as adults from kids. But you can, can't you?'

'Look at some of the kids we know. The ones we know just because we grew up with their parents. We encourage them to be naughty.' They both point to each other in agreement, laughing.

'We're the ones who will defend them when they fail school or don't come home, or whatever their drug will be.'

'I actually secretly hope we'll be the ones they'll run away to when they're older.'

'That's a bit wishful isn't it? We'll be too old by then.'

People stroll past their window table at the Bourbon and Beefsteak Bar on Darlinghurst road where they're having a late breakfast, starting with Bloody Marys.

'I don't know. What made you question it all?'

'Sex, I'd say.' She goes into peals of laughter. Her friend giggles.

'It's true.'

Their lightly poached eggs arrive looking like bleached wrinkled scrotums. They both pass the same look at each other and order two more Bloody Marys. The golden yellow yolks stain through and around the toast and the slices of tomato as they tuck into the hash browns.

'Tomato and eggs are an uncomfortable combination. Red water and yellow fat don't mix. Tomatoes make eggs look common and eggs make tomatoes look plain.'

'Do you ever think whether they're from battery hens or not?'

'Not really.'

'I had this guy staying with me once who was into natural

121

food. He'd buy half a dozen free-range eggs – six would cost twice as much as a dozen ordinary ones. And he didn't have much money. Well, actually he was saving while staying with me. He was earning enough. I hate people who have no generosity, don't you?' Their drinks arrive.

'I did something one day when he wasn't home. I ate all his eggs and replaced them with ones from the corner shop. Next morning when I came down he was having breakfast. Those eggs look nice, I said. Hmm, he said. You can really taste the difference.'

'Did you tell him?'

'You're joking,' she says. 'But I told everyone else.'

STRANGERS

It may have seemed like grabbing a moment of happiness with this new friend, but it wasn't. Nor was it romance. It didn't even have anything to do with love. If anything, it was gambling with love, but with a difference. So for a week he allowed his lover to estrange himself to a beach on the South Coast. He did nothing to encourage him to go away, but equally he did nothing to interfere. It wasn't a timid response. It was practical.

'If that's what you want to do then do it. But there's really no need to.'

And his lover had replied in a controlled way but with no false ease, 'I'd rather not have to keep going home knowing that you'll be sleeping with someone else.'

Listening then to the response being formed, rapidly, deliberately, he avoided picking up on the hints of jealousy and rancour that would surface later when his lover returned home and rang him.

No introduction. No hello. No how are you. Just a simple statement of being back.

'It's me here.'

A simple statement full of heartache, full of thinking. Too full. Too full of imagined fantasies. Seven days away from the city to brood thickly and quietly. Then to relax. But in the last day, in that last hour to find yourself returning in a furnace of hate.

Returned. Yelling over the phone. Of wickedness, betrayal, of laughing behind his back, of the indignity in front of his friends, of the loss of self-esteem. No, no reassurance, just punishment. That was the point – to go away to the beach in Austinmer with no intention of reprisal, to wait out the arranged time, then to return and hit out.

That's how it came about that his lover evaporated and he slept for five days with a young guy from Melbourne. And it wasn't romance. It wasn't even sexual. They didn't fuck, though everyone assumed that they did.

Everyone who knew about it assumed night pleasures. Humping and moaning, souls touching each other, lips trembling and two bodies begging, hugging, convulsed in a perfect union. Fucking together. Doing each other, again and again. Wanting each other more than anyone had ever wanted ever before.

Loud fucking noises. Grunts of languidness, spacious noises, easy-going somersaulting in the air full of casual laughter, abandoned rests, eyes closed, which led again to reaching into the pockets of the body, his body or mine, anything and everything, a mad clamour, the vagueness of a force that only too much involvement, too much strain of fast-hitting sex can release out of control. And then a moment later, together, reaching for a cigarette. The stuff that jealousy is made of.

But none of this happened.

Not that there weren't sexual moments, moments which led them, almost always individually but from different motives, to retreat into a private fixation. Little distances. Tiny thoughtful moments. Pivotal stances a hair-breadth away from indifference would intervene, would push them apart. But only for a moment, after which the placid balance, the accepted distance between them both would fix and equalise into a spacious harmony again.

One moment was when he said, 'Don't you find me sexually attractive?' And the other had replied, 'You know how it always is. The people who are attracted to you don't usually interest you. And your perfect sex objects don't care much for you either.'

He thought about this as he turned around in bed and put his arm around his new friend and kissed him gently in the hollow of his back. The other, responding, moved to accommodate this person sleeping close against him, his flesh so warm, moving to avoid the jut of his arm or the bone of his elbow or a knee jammed too firmly against his muscles, tired now with wanting to sleep. The slight withdrawals and juxtapositions, the half-conscious movements flowing from a natural relaxation that spurs you into a blanketed rest. And then later, no longer awake but only moments before sleep, before the separation of dreaming, when they moved apart and turned over into themselves, they both granted a touch against each other, a small feeling touch, and fell carefully into sleep, the warm cheeks of their bums cementing this sometime of being together.

At first when he told his lover of his friend's arrival, he thought his lover was over-reacting.

'It's not as if I'm going to live with him. He's only here for a few days.'

And his lover had pointed out, 'That's how things always start.'

It was true. But in this instance all he could say was, 'But

127

you've always refused to live with me.'

They were their last words for seven days. Then his lover returned and rang him. And their last words followed close on.

────────

He woke, momentarily disoriented.

He'd woken in the wrong place. He knew it by the direction of the morning light. Or was it midday already?

Startled, he moved quickly, sat upright. For an instant he was more confused than ever.

A small flicker of panic creased him as he looked around the brightly lit room. But his fear faded as he recognised where he was. The sound of the sea rolling in reminded him of the black cormorants waiting on the beach below, sitting on the posts, forever watching. He almost felt a temptation to check if there was anyone else with him, but he knew he was alone. That's the price you pay.

Readjusting the cotton sheet over his body, he lay back on the bed and pushed one knee up, stretching the lethargy of another night of drinking out of his muscles. Another night of serious drinking. But it wasn't amusing.

'I'm a sucker for circumstances,' he thought to himself, not without self-pity. Anything was appropriate now. Even the truth, whatever it was, except he knew the truth only too well.

He'd needed distance, so he'd left Sydney. He needed time, so he waited. For how long? You couldn't make plans. But it had to be long enough to wrench a lover from your system.

The overwhelming strength of his bitterness shook him. He almost convulsed but he forced himself to retain control as he twisted the hurt out and replaced it with hatred. Then he felt sick with love.

'I must stop fucking up,' he confided to himself. 'Just keep soldiering on.'

128

The split had been a long time coming. The relationship had been busting around the edges for years. For two years it had been stupendously fine, then five years of mounting misery punctuated by moments of remission. Had he not seen the signs? Of course he had. But he was rapt in the guy. Then everything had happened in a day. Busting up for real this time.

The terror that gripped him at that breaking moment was beyond any feeling. The only thing left was a need for movement, a drive to get out.

He found he had to flee, run, hide. But he put the decision off for twenty-four hours, hoping. No reason. Just hoping. And when the telephone call had not come, hour after hour, through a dull afternoon and a restless night and a dazzling morning, by mid-morning he knew it was time to run away.

So he did.

He packed a briefcase full of books. In another bag he folded a towel, shorts, sun-screen lotion, pens, a jumper, two pairs of jeans, socks for three days, all his underwear, his address book, vitamins and his diary. He packed his friends he could rely on, his family, some money and a bank book. His wasted days, his happy thoughts, his washed-out feelings, his caustic love, he left all this behind. He rearranged his packages, straightened them out, made his bed, cut the crap and left.

And now here he was, half a Valium and fifteen minutes later, feeling more comfortable, confident almost. He reached for a glass of water by the bed, but it was empty. The spark of life sent rattled messages of protest which he obeyed.

As he walked into the kitchen he glanced at the clock. It was six. Funny, he thought. The world collapses around you, your emotions convulse, you spend all your time drinking too much and smoking too much dope, which fucks you up even further, and what's the end result? You wake in the morning, register the time, have a piss, check out what's around you, get some water, make a coffee, everything so revoltingly, predictably normal.

How timid you feel without a lover after you have had one.

I have hit the time of promiscuous negligence. I dreamed this morning that I was at a party. There were lots of people there I didn't know. All of you weren't there. All of you who have been held inside my legs. Who are in my mind. Who were in my bed. Who are still in my present thoughts. No dreams can wake me out of that.

Dreams are stupid things, the mud thoughts of a mind at rest rearranging the cells of feeling. Vigorously, while dreaming, I discard the holes in my life. Some people disappear on bottles of emptiness, projectiles shot off into the dust of the past, wine casks drained of everything. And some my mind chooses to throw away with less trace, like a pen poised above a dried-out ink well, a metaphor for a person well remembered but worth nothing more. Further than a garbage bin.

The mind plays funny tricks. It is a world unto itself. Like snoring. You fall asleep, but the sounds you make go walking regardless of your wishes. Walking all over the world of your life. Teasing you with false profundity.

None of you were with me last night. No one was here. Just a late winter storm in October. Sydney in the spring. A quick downpour. A quick demand. A sip of wine, a meal, an empty bottle, a quick goodbye, a look around, gone, sudden rain, a sudden stop. He's driving in a car to the ocean, getting closer to home, ozone in the air, chablis on the brain, rain banging on my windows and lightning over Paddington, travelling to Bondi and out to sea while I am asleep, restlessly tossing, wakened from dreaming again and alone, alarmed by the images of the dream, the fearful furies of the night, and thoughts of you, whoever you were.

You, like an asteroid falling. You, like moss covering my

sheets. You, like my head wrapped in plastic, like bathroom mould, like sunburn, like jelly beans, like ambergris, like broken crystal, a styptic pencil, like an insect catcher, like a war-time grave.

I'm not to blame if I spend the rest of the night drinking my writer's whisky, trying to put into words the feeling I have about living without him and the one before him, alone, not sleeping with anyone, not sleeping at all.

'It is not loneliness,' I write. 'It is a feeling of not knowing what to do.'

——————

The Eastern Suburbs train travels around the edge of Rushcutters Bay Park on its journey to Bondi Junction. I see its vague slithering from the window of my work-room flat in Elizabeth Bay, the lighted windows of its carriages appearing and disappearing behind the grove of trees around the oval.

Six months ago I would have been on that train ready to catch the bus to Bondi Beach. To see a man, of course. A man first noticed, then introduced to, seen for a moment to arrange a meeting, then to be entranced by. To kiss, to seduce, to sleep with for a night. To come back, be invited back, to become a lover, fucked, wanted, hugged, enamoured, obsessed by. Only then, to become choked when, as a slow loser, this lover turned first into a soul mate, then best friend, then true friend, then just friend, then hurtful friend, then someone I know well, knew well, an acquaintance. Then someone remembered, reminded of. Then a piece of history met every once in a while by a forgotten me.

After our last meeting he said to me, 'It was a fling. It's over now. You take these things so seriously. I tried to think it might work. It didn't. I couldn't get serious.' He bites his lip as he says this. I know he is lying.

PRIVATE – DO NOT OPEN

It is eight months since I last slept with my ex-lover. Ironically, my ex-lover now lives in the building next door with his present boyfriend. The irony is not one of proximity as most of our friends see it, for we almost never run into each other. The irony is that seven years ago, when I lived in that same block of flats and our bodies pined for each other, I said to him, 'Why don't you live with me?'

And he replied, 'Not yet. It is too soon. I'm not ready for that yet. Wait till the time is right, when I'm ready. The time will come. Be patient. Don't push too quickly. It'll turn out okay. Just let me get used to the idea slowly. It will happen.' I let the time pass. Seven years. It turned out to be wilful destruction. So I pissed him off. I replaced him with someone who did the same.

I know many friends who have become attached to their solitary homes scattered everywhere throughout Sydney, quietly drinking red wine or smoking dope by themselves, thinking –

BONDI: 'I've never really lived with anyone in my life. It has always been a matter of staying with them at their place or they at mine. A shared common living with a lover is a myth in my life.'

ELIZABETH BAY: 'We've all spent a million more times by ourselves than we have with other people. That's an exaggeration, but you know what I mean. And yet we all imagine that somehow it should have been different. It's the waiting that's the problem. Do you ever find yourself doing nothing?'

KINGS CROSS: 'I cannot comprehend living with someone after those first six weeks of obsessive lust. I don't like habit. I hate questions of money, careers, breakfast. After a while I hate it when someone else is there.'

PADDINGTON: 'I feel so insecure that I put too much meaning into everything. And I know it's not true, but I feel unattractive.'

BALMAIN: 'I'm tempted to call it sadness, but I never allow

132

those sorts of feelings to dominate me. It's more a matter of being realistic. But then, when I think about what has happened in my life, truly, I would never have predicted any of this. It's not that I don't like it, and it's not as if I've been disappointed. It has more to do with the fact that we expected something different.'

NEWTOWN: 'Those young things. They've never had their hearts broken. So they never know what pain they cause when they break yours.'

STANMORE: 'I'm terrified that people might think that I have no pride. I'm terrified that people will think of me as desperate. Which is the same as saying you're stupid.'

HABERFIELD: 'I don't try any more. I sit back and observe what others do, watch them entangle each other. Then I go home. If you hear of any good parties, ring me.'

A common silence has bitten into our shared solitude. And yet, in our search for human warmth, the momentary pleasures of the flesh, the needs of sex and friendships, of love and talking frankly, despite this, we continue to accumulate a store of strangers. The friends of the future, if they last.

LAST DRINK IS ON THE HOUSE

. . . and then it was ten years later.

How did they all fit in and how many of them were there feeling that they all belonged together and was it even correct to bring them in under the same heading, some of them didn't like one another and some of them were so oppositely different (some were dead) and some had not been seen for years, not since the big unruly Builders Labourers' marches dead set through the heart of Sydney streets saying that they were never prepared to forgive or forget or lose, which they did (kind of). No, I know. It was 1975 when they dragged themselves out to the pro-Whitlam rallies marching with the Eastern Suburbs Labor branches, convinced that the Working Men and Women of Australia would not stand for this, which of course they did. (Some of us slept in of course, pursuing

137

another kind of politics.)

Must be over ten years now since the Newcastle Hotel in Lower George Street closed its bar and then its doors for the last time, forever on 23 February 1973, and locked up some people's ability to think straight, which was one of the things Sydney pubs did. (Even Wendy cried when the Newcastle closed, though that could have been earlier when the pub just closed for the night.) And Pyrmont Bridge now closed too. A shocking vengeance on those of us who waited in taxis (Sydney's were the cheapest) for the bridge to swing open while on our way to the London Hotel in Balmain (always on Saturday afternoon) or a party in someone's backyard. Let me tell you, even ten years ago parts of the inner city were almost rural. Backyards you could hold a proper party in. For 400 people, not like today. I hear there's a new set of drinkers at the London who are meant to be okay, but I can't believe that. They're not our set, different arguments. Such are the times. Such are the winds of city living. Even Darcy's moved away as lots of them have. Moved on. Written books or made films, or so we'd like to believe, or married and made children. There are probably more who have had babies and who now send them to proper schools (private) where they hope they won't pick up drug habits (like their parents, my friends, did) or turn out to be lesbians. They might anyway. (I can remind you of who you fucked when you were younger, if you've forgotten. I know people I can ask.)

It's funny drinking with the kids of the people we grew up drinking with. Only the haircuts have changed (so we'd like to think). And the drinks – Kahlua and milk now. Them at drinking age ('What do you do?' 'I go to school.') Past puberty, fucking, sometimes for lust, sometimes just because that's what you end up doing. Nothing changes much.

Listen. 'The number of nights that ended up with the obligatory poke after the pub. I don't remember who half of them were, *most* of them. You didn't enjoy it, you just did it. I don't think anyone told me it was meant to be good. But that was the late fifties early sixties. God's teeth, twenty years of drink smoke poke, drink smoke poke. Who'd want to do that again?'

Their children of course. Whose mother's weren't widgees, so they now wear black and have a no-face white make-up and red lipstick so dark it's brown and smoke cigarettes because they're harmful (that's why we started smoking too) and hang around saying, 'It's too depressing really.' It was always too depressing. When your entertainment boiled down to reading someone's personality based on what colour Cocktail Sobranie they chose – pink and acquamarine were the best, though straw was more interesting. The basics never change.

When you haven't got enough money to get home, you don't go home. You bludge. Cigarettes, whisky, a Greek meal of egg-plant cooked too long and a garlic dip and bread and oil and everyone drinking Retsina and calling it furniture polish and yelling at each other about politics (the Greeks closed in 1985) and I did *not* say that, you don't ever listen. I said that men on the Left are fucked. They're fucked! You still expect women to do all the shitwork and then turn into a mother in bed while you get over your insecurities. And then you men get up in the morning and do the dishes, so how bloody wonderful that you do them, taking precious time off your work because its too early to make phone calls or pick your suit up from the dry cleaners. Well I'm not waiting for your revolution until things become more tolerable for me because I'm thirty-six and I want it now and fuck all of you, what am I meant to do? because I'm pregnant and I haven't got £50 (later two hundred dollars and later still a signature on a Medibank form not that the abortions changed much) and so someone would have to win on the races the next Saturday (always on the last race they say) and you're never expected to pay the money back because everyone's forgotten or it's only money and should flow around to be spent or is it guilt? you'll never know. Because everyone talks on, have you got enough money to buy

me a drink? and they hand you a fiver and never expect to see
the change, and it's not like charity because it's always an
offer you can't refuse, and you go over to the bar and buy what
they always drink and a drink for yourself and the money
which now disappears becomes someone else's. You always
carry as much as you can afford to spend even in a catastrophe.
That's why if you didn't have any you'd still go and ask, even
a total stranger. That's one way how we got to know each
other. It was a kind of crime to be rich but never a crime to be
poor.

How did we all first get there, to a pub like the Dry Dock? Also
closed, swept away by the mysterious whirlwind of time. Like
the Royal George or the Purple Onion or the Hasty Tasty or
who can remember Repins or even Madame Fiasci's? The Dry
Dock, off Darling Street then off another street and around the
corner and you could easily miss it if it wasn't for the dead end
of the Balmain docks that were even then coming up from
working class. Coming up for air. Raising children who would
alter Australian politics, a suburb being transformed.
Workers' cottages made liveable again. Nine-foot frontages
with sixty-foot backyards (subdivided before we could stop
them with Green Bans in the mid-nineteenth century),
another inner-city suburb of that rich lazy languid magnificent corruptedly beguiling crowded dirty polluted shimmering harbour city of Sydney, that shameless brazen jewelled
metropolis that gave itself too abundantly to the imagination
of money, too abruptly, so much so that the first white imperi-
alists landing on its shore almost starved for fifty years before
they cottoned onto corruption. Built the Rum Hospital, now
Parliament House. No pissing there on the restored sandstone
steps of Macquarie Street, like we could do in Chippendale,
Redfern, the Rocks and Woolloomooloo whose pubs spilled out
onto the streets paved with drunks swilling their booze and
pissing in back lanes, themselves the last remnants of a time

(not all that long ago) of latrines and the weekly collection of night soil. It's funny how people in Sydney still piss in the street, squat in a gutter, splatter behind a tree. And a fuck's just that a fuck. Love is reserved for the people you want to know better. Who you met ten or twenty years ago at a pub which no longer stands.

This is not history. This is tradition.

'Oh no, we won't go,' she sang drunk in the gutter by the Royal Oak in Chippendale after being turfed out after closing time. 'Oh no, we won't go.' That was Gillian. It must have been a Thursday because we always drank there on a Thursday or had we started going to the Eveleigh Hotel called the Evil Eye because you were never sure when it was to be your turn to be thrown out for doing nothing. Maybe just trying to play pool. One moment the management (that's how she learned to call herself) would be apologising for not having a colour TV and then the next refusing to serve smarty-pants intellectuals who wanted a round of unheard-of sophisticated drinks, Parfait Amour doo you mind and a colour TV and pool balls all over the floor (after the cues had been confiscated to prevent imaginary fights). Well if you don't like it get out because we don't serve the likes of you, we're an old-fashioned corner hotel which doesn't stock expensive drinks. No, the scotch is off – what's wrong with beer? Did you hear the way he spoke to me? I'm not having any of that sort of talk in my pub. Fuck. Before you had time to find the money in your pocket the bar would be closed and the lights off and if you tried to be reasonable you got a stare that packed the punch of a swift kick. I said the bar's closed and you lot are banned. Don't let me see you in here again. And the next time (after a week) she'd be your most intimate friend bemoaning that no one drank there anymore and please come again and bring your friends. We don't pretend to be anything special and some pubs don't but we like young people here, it gives the place some life. Sorry there's no colour TV but the place is friendly don't you think? Late one night someone pulled a knife though I personally didn't see this. There was a woman sitting in the lounge shelling peas. No one was barred that night. I don't think anyone sang that we won't go at the Evil Eye. Or maybe we did. Fact and fiction can get muddled when you're trying to write down so many things about so many people's lives, not to mention the huge amounts of alcohol consumed on every page.

'Oh no, we won't go down no more
Oh no, we won't go down no more
Stars are rolling in and out of my ears
Stars are rolling in and out of my ears
Oh they roll in and out
Make me want to jump and shout
Oh no, we won't go down no more.'

(The Evil Eye has gone gay now.)

Sitting in our bedrooms after the annual pub crawl, drunkedly cutting our nails, concentrating on the country and western music coming from next door, the sound of washing up from someplace else, the light on through the jacaranda trees opposite your window – people we don't know except that they walk quicky past their window sometimes semi-naked and play piano late at night, the beat of jazz piano, annoyingly late for some of the residents occupying identical nine-foot frontage terraces ('I live in a house two-foot too wide, it's a pleasant old house on the Newtown Side . . .'). Then Stewart or Jill announcing something on 2JJJ radio followed by a Triffids record and we know someone who used to mix for that band. The planes flying overhead coming in too late too loud, breaking the curfew and causing the academic who lives slightly closer to the flight path in Petersham to continue to record her register of complaints for eventual submission to the ombudsperson. A troublemaker like most of us.

Then things get quieter, people go to bed. But the jittery dogs remain, barking like vigilantes. And the whining whingeing ever-present cat population skulking and preying, protecting their territorial rights from lord knows what threat. An occasional late-coming car. Then silence. A long drinking smoking reflective silence, the meandering quiet sounds of an occasional drunk stepping home in a muffled unsureness. If you stay up long enough – dawn. The quick clicking of stiletto shoes running against the indefinable call of close-distanced noises reminiscent of nothing else except early morning in a big city, a rising general hum two suburbs away, the slow introduction of another day. Shift-workers arriving home for breakfast. Early starters revving the motors of their cars before speeding off to the first rays of the sun. And the bustling burly bad-mouthed garbage collectors slamming their abuse at stray cats lounging on the road and at the occupants of houses asleep down my way.

Here they come. Past the artists, past someone we don't know, past the drug-addict recluse, past Jeff's – you can hear the beer bottles, past Sue's – hear the flagons? past the christians – cardboard boxes, past the trendy new couple we don't like – black plastic garbage bags, big full ones that fall open with illegal home-renovation debris. Why don't you put proper garbage out? yells the rubbish man and those of us awake enough to hear this nod our approval as the compressor yawns and pounds, banging the refuse of our neighbourhood into a neat disposable block. Then another bin and another, then mine, loud with bottles and the previous night's dinner with friends (mainly bottles). And then you truly know it's time for bed. Otherwise if you stay up much longer you'll start making sleepless connections between community and garbage.

Falling asleep to someone walking down creaking stairs next door.

Falling asleep to the milk being delivered to the corner shop and the paper-girl blowing her whistle, stopping to sell or thump a bundle into the balcony.

Teachers leaving for school.

Falling asleep while school kids mark your fence or make delinquent sounds with bits of wood on the cast-iron railings. KEVIN IS A PENCIL-CASE SNITCHER – TRUE written in biro, and underneath in pencil, CHERYL IS A MOLE.

Falling asleep thinking of things to be done tomorrow which is already here.

Falling asleep where you belong.

Time was the essence of it all. The time that just happened to be right. It's wrong to say we were there. *There* was where we weren't. That was the attraction.

They pulled us off the streets those drinkers in those pubs. And then we ended up drinking on those same streets. There was no need for introductions and there was no indoctrination. We heard about those places like we heard about sex. Clandestine knowledge. They weren't like strangers waiting for us – we ran into their arms like drug addicts to heroin, like writers to computers, like the poor to money, like thieves to property, like children to god (there were always some that went wrong). It was something we had to have, though what we ran to and what we were running from were two different things by then.

'Why don't we ever see each other more often? We've known one another for so long. Sure, the world changes. So do we. Our friends are strangers to each other. It's been like that for years. But we, we've known ourselves develop together. You know? grow up, mature. (THE FIRST PROOF OF EXISTENCE IS TO OCCUPY SPACE.) I suppose it was different then. We were younger, full of idealism, full of disrespect. We loved to make a bit of scandal (I almost feel I shouldn't say this, but I loved those times, looking back.)

144

'We were in the vanguard of the opposition then, sitting down before the cops, feeling revolutionary. (WHOEVER YOU VOTE FOR, A POLITICIAN STILL GETS IN.) Demand the impossible – I believed in all that. Still do. They were the only reasons we taunted the cops into arresting us. I wasn't brave. Nor were any of us. We were just young and careless, with a few ideas. Remember fronting court? And then we went and had a drink together at the Criterion. There was a spirit then. (IF YOU CAN READ AND WRITE YOU CAN TOWN PLAN – AND EVEN IF YOU CAN'T YOU CAN.) It was nice. It was nice and real. We believed in something. Don't ask me what it was, I'd say I can't remember except – we stuck to each other. We did. Maybe that was all it was. I can't fathom it all now. Maybe the times were different. But it was something, we had something, and I miss those times.'

The times are different. We are now strangers to our former selves, let alone to those of us we know.

Reg went off and had a baby.

David married his childhood sweetheart and now feels embarrassed when he meets me.

Ian is a successful economist. He's now in a position to fire people (he does).

Lynn inherited a fortune when her father died.

Laura became a prostitute.

No one knows what happened to Fran, though Susan interviewed her for a job (secretary) and said she was hopeless.

Susan's working in the Women's Unit (State Government).

Carl fled the country and died in a freak accident.

Richard OD'd on smack, no one even knew he was using.

Betty still drinks in pubs.

Caroline went mad, but she's out of the bin now.

Peter went to New York to make it big in films. He works there now in a men's wear store.

Gail is still a teacher (she's learning Arabic).

Lance finished Law (some say he's corrupt).
Brett and Ian are in jail.
Wendy got born again (so did Nigel, but it didn't last).
Andrew's still gay.
Madeline is a lesbian separatist and still hates men.
Kelvin, always a bit of a hippy, lives in northern NSW on a commune.
John keeps getting grants.
Jan hates everybody (she never even sees her oldest friends).
Deidre lost her baby when Michael left her (some would say she was lucky).
Marian married a policeman (the worst thing anyone could do).
Bronwyn reads the news on television.
Ken won't live with his lover (I feel trapped, he says).
Meredith keeps laughing about her fate.
Most people have forgotten about Chris (he's dead anyway).
Liz and Robert keep falling for young things.
Marion still cries. (When will I see him again? *I Ching*, 17 and 49, 'following revolution.')

She staggers in late, slipping into her street anonymously late, like all those other gregarious solitary drunks around Chippendale. Secretly (shhh). All stationed by their front doors holding tightly to the keys which are their only source of support. By the front door needing help, scratching determinedly at the lock (I can see it but it won't go in) trying to find a way of opening that magic door to home.
Then suddenly the key turns and she's in.
'Hooray!' she yells (shh) and slams the door. Followed by staring into the dark (I know where I am) followed by a quiet foot-feeling shuffle, edging along, feeling for some object (should be soon) . . . what's next? (She'll fall over the

couch in a moment.)

'Hey, you up there! Where's the light?' And over she goes, over the couch and onto the floor, slowly sprawling (drunk), catching herself from falling by a bit of fabric, mumbling, 'Could have left the lights on, the bugger.' Finds the wall, climbs it, hands feeling for the switch, the light, finds it, lights on (hooray!) then back to the floor for a well-earned rest and a few good-mood chuckles. But there's more crawling to be done yet.

'Where's my ...' She stops, then starts again, louder this time. 'Where's my Bessie Smith record?' She tries to sound inspired, then a little more pragmatically (lying down) says, 'And my gin?' She lies quietly for a full four seconds. This is when the crawling really begins.

'Hey you up there (hic), where's Bessie's gin eh?'

I'm up now (of course) out of bed and my pants are almost on. My head is laid skew-wiff on its alcoholic sleepy side where it's been for a passed-out hour and you come in like this, like tomorrow's flagon-breaking mattress-hugging hangover. Stop yelling for god's sake you drunken oaf, I'm coming. I manage to pop my shoulders and head around the corner upside down from the top of the stairs looking like an unathletic drunk, which I am, and say, 'You lost it, remember?' I try to sound soberly compassionate.

'I know (hic). But I can still hope can't I?' She opens her eyes off the floor. I make it to the bottom of the stairs, slipping a bit.

There's a word in Russian. It means something like a voice that's been ruined by too much hard liquor and too many cigarettes. When she learnt of it she began to smoke and drink more. To achieve a closer spiritual equivalent (hic) you understand? Of course you do.

'I'm drunk,' she confides. 'How about you?'

'I've been asleep so I don't feel so good,' I say.

'A couple more glasses is what we need.' The inference is not lost on me.

147

Creme de Cacao. It's the last alcohol left in the house.

'Perfect,' she says, smiling through her nose.

After half a bottle we're both up staggering around looking for Bessie, where are you Bessie, I love that record, it's my favourite, my most favourite and now she's dead and I've lost the record.

'No one can understand anything unless they've had gin. Have you had gin?' She pauses, waiting, then turns her head to one side onto her shoulder, takes a puff of her cigarette and as she blows the smoke out languidly says, 'I have.'

We've found the cooking brandy which we'd hidden from ourselves in case of an emergency exactly like this. We pour each other a measured drop and Sue starts her story.

'I used to know this guy once who collected newspapers.'

'You're making this up.'

'No I'm not,' she says seriously. 'This is all perfectly true. I knew this guy who collected newspapers.' She laughs, admiring the thought.

'Anyway. He'd wander around all day finding the news-papers.' (Drink, sip, splash.)

'Why didn't he buy them?'

'He couldn't. That wasn't allowed. He had to find them. That was the game. He had to go around finding all the different editions.' She lights another cigarette. So do I.

'He studied history. He was probably crazy.'

I don't believe a word. 'How do you know? Did you fuck him?'

'Once,' she says, reacting boldly. She kicks her shoe off up at the wall. It hits and leaves a mark.

I challenge her. 'Where?'

'In the gutter.' It might be true, the way she punctuates her words.

'Anyway (hic). He'd cart them home, all the newspapers he'd collected that day. And some of them are really dirty, like

148

he hadn't been able to get another copy of that particular one so a dirty one had to do. Have you got the brandy?'

'How did he earn his money?'

'I think he was on the dole, but I don't know for sure. He lived in that house next to where Pam and Elizabeth used to live.'

'The one that got burned down?'

'Do you want to hear the story or don't you? Well shut up then!' She drinks another shot. 'He must have got money from somewhere, but I don't know where. Anyway. He'd bring all the papers home, and you know what he'd do? He'd iron them.' She gets bad hiccoughs.

'He'd iron them,' she says, 'with an iron (hic). I have to have a piss. Wait till I get back.'

As the toilet's flushing she says, 'Where (hic) was I up to?'

'You fucked him in the gutter.'

'We were past that. He was ironing. He ironed them. And some he even washed.' The fantasy is still alive, as are the hiccoughs.

'Try Pam's sugar cure,' I yell to her (Three spoonfulls of sugar eaten straight).

'Well time gets on and he's been doing this for a year by this time and he's got papers all round his house' (She's standing by the kitchen door eating sugar, hic). 'Not just lying in a mess but all neat and tidy. Like a library. All catalogued and put in their right places.'

She waits two minutes as Pam's cure works. Then we both rush to have a drink again.

'I don't think he ever read them,' she says. 'He just collected them. And they were piled right up the walls. Some rooms you couldn't get into, they were full of newspapers.'

As she comes back into the lounge, she looks up and wonders if the shoe mark on the wall will wash off. 'Who cares,' she mumbles, then settles back onto the floor. After a pause she continues, talking at the ceiling.

'He had this philosophy, and he used to say to people in a really slow heavy way when people asked him what he was doing (she puts on her best patriarchal voice), 'People THINK, that if you Produce, a *lot* of Things, you know, Mass Produce Things, that it's *almost certain* that at least SOME of those Things will *survive* into the Future. But History had proved him right. The ephemeral object, the Ephemeral Object was less likely to *survive* because people knew there were lots of them, so they didn't mind throwing things out, like it wouldn't matter if they did because someone else would keep their's. And that's why nothing would survive of our time and history proved this.' Her impersonation has dropped with the aptness of this insight.

'So! He, this guy, had taken it upon himself to make sure that newspapers at least would survive.' She laughs again, aghast in admiration. 'I think that's terrific.' (Small thinking pause.)

'And you know what he called himself?' This is the climax. 'THE LEADER OF THE HISTORICAL REPOSITORY OF HIS OWN AGE.'

We are both aghast (the brandy's finished).

'Is that the end?'

'No. There's a bit more.' She sits up. We both sit up.

'I don't see him for about a year and then, I think it was Xmas day, and I've got no idea how he got my phone number. But he rings me up and says, can I come over? It's urgent.' She tries her drink which is empty.

'I told him to piss off and hung up.' She giggles, squeezing a last drop from the brandy bottle. (One drop drips out.)

'So he calls back and says, my house has burnt down.' The last dribble gets finished.

'What could I do? I said, all right. Come over but bring a flagon.'

Silence.

'Oh, boy!' She remembers something.

DETAILS, BEFORE THE EVENT

I am waiting for a cab. I've left work early to spend some time away and by myself, which I spend in the Rest Hotel drinking red wine and reading about Kurt Schwitters. And after two hours, I just decide to take my thoughts and leave. Get down to serious matters.

The first cab takes a radio call just as I hail it. So I stand on the street waiting. Milson's Point, the north end of the Bridge, too rich by day when the advertising execs, all of them either twenty-five or fifty, dominate the streets. But after dark, after their few drinks at the local, before going off somewhere flash (but probably home), these pieces of useless capital disappear.

I am not sure that the man behind me who was waiting as I arrived is not also watching for a cab. It isn't generosity but fair play that makes me ask, 'Are you waiting for a taxi?' 'No,

153

mate,' he says. He is holding five heavily-laden plastic bags.
The bags are clean and new, so I don't pick him for a bag man.
We stand for a while while a couple of private cars go by. Then
blandly he asks, 'You wouldn't have a spare forty cents on you,
would you?'

'Sure,' I say, pulling out some change. 'I hope I have,'

There's a dollar there, which I give him, adding, 'I hope
you've got enough now.'

'Would you like some bread back?' he asks. For a moment I
think he's offering me change, till he adds, 'I work for a baker.'
He lifts his five bags and I understand. They're full of
yesterday's white sliced bread.

'Thanks,' I say, but add quickly, 'I don't eat bread.'

'Quick,' he points. 'There's a vacant cab over there.' As we
run across the road together, the cab driver gets out of his car
and looks to be heading into the pub.

'Are you vacant?' I ask.

'As soon as I've bought some more cigarettes,' says the driver
and heads into the pub along with the bread carrier who says,
'See you,' to me. I get into the cab.

In a minute the driver returns. I tell him I want to go to
Bondi. 'I wonder if I can turn here without being caught?' he
says to me, looking up and down the street. He decides it's safe
and makes a U-turn. As we pull away, the bread man comes out
of the pub with a bottle wrapped in newspaper and waves to
me. I wave back.

'Which way do you want to go?' asks the driver. 'I don't care,
you're the driver,' I say. 'Whichever way you want.'

'Don't really make any difference,' he repeats twice. 'You
get people who pretend to know which way's shorter, and they
end up saving forty cents. What can you buy for forty cents
these days?'

At the intersection of Crown and William Streets,
Woolloomooloo, he stops halfway up the hill to allow the
driver in front to reverse. They are both making way for a

garbage truck cornered in a small side street. The garbage truck driver waves as he clears the street and turns.

I notice that there's a full moon as we speed along the Edgecliff freeway. And that Sydney again looks clean and sparkling after this afternoon's sub-tropical downpour.

As the cab pulls into my street and alongside my house, I unbuckle my seat-belt and say to the driver, 'I've just got to get some money from inside.' I leave my bags and my diary on the front seat, just in case. 'Take your time,' says the driver, turning off the meter. I go inside to get some of next week's rent. Jan and Tim come out of the house. As they leave, they wave. 'Where are you off to?' I ask. 'Down the road.' The Bondi wind blows the rest of their reply away.

At home, Di is in bed watching TV. 'How are you?' I say, coming into her room. 'You look well.' Di has just had her cervix lasered after a positive Pap smear.

'You look really well,' I say, which she does.

'I know,' she says, laughing. 'I feel really guilty taking this week off work and feeling great.' That's not how she felt two days ago after coming back from hospital, angry and sore, and pale.

'You look really awful,' I say. 'I think you need to take a holiday.'

'Yeah,' she says, cigarette in hand. 'I think I do need to go away,' she agrees, smiling. 'Down the South Coast for a few days.'

Little details, a day no different to any other day in my life. Except that I am in love and it's tearing me apart.

I am in love and I hate it.

———————

How can one reconstruct someone's personal history when you don't know all the details? Imagination. That's one reply.

That's the writer's craft. Make it seem real, as if it could happen. So your readers will believe it did. A portrait of the time.

Pam says to me today over breakfast (both of us suffering a hangover tiredness, a portrait of our time), 'I don't write fiction. I write non-fiction. Nuclear physics has become fiction these days.' We all agree. Then we all talk about how the papers said that the hijacking of the Egyptian airliner was staged by Iraq. Not that anyone really knew.

I sit and read the newspaper for a while, then turn to Pam and say, 'I feel as if I've had a kip.'

'I'm not surprised, reading the *Sydney Morning Herald*.'

Ken and Ken, two painters, talk throughout about people who have thrown care to the wind and run away. About people who have lived in caves, who have fled to the jungle and on returning, fled there again.

'He sailed a boat to Timor from Australia in the fifties,' says Ken. 'It was front page in all the newspapers. And when they brought him back to Australia, he set off again. A barrel of pork and a barrel of water.' I mishear this as a barrel of port and a barrel of water. 'And went off to Bribie Island to live in a sunken ship. He was called the rear admiral. Later he hauled the guts of a plane over, shot down during the second world war. He lived and painted in there for the rest of his life.

'There weren't many people in the deadened fifties in Australia after the war who tried to do anything different. There were a few, a precious few. I was young then, in my twenties. I went to a few of Rowie Norton's parties in the Cross. Harry Hooton, I never met him. But John Sillett, a friend of Hooton's, he was living in a boat shed in Musgrave Street in Mosman. One night he threw all his books into the harbour. All writing is an evil, he said as he did it. I was shocked, but delighted. I was in my early twenties then and here was this man throwing his whole library into the water because of Civilisation. I said, but what about Jesus Christ? I was young you understand, and here was a real person, in Australia. All he said was, look at what his words have done.

'He changed his name to Nozmo King.'

'No Smoking,' says Pam. 'I like that,' she says, smoking.

Ken, the older painter, has run away.

Ken, the younger drinker, painter, also has.

'I might go and live in a cave,' says Pam, who has often run away over the past ten years.

After five minutes I say, 'Well, I have to go to work,' and leave. I don't seem capable of running away. Not like that, anyway.

––––––––––

It is absolutely of no importance to talk about this, yet everyone feels this – that you can never explain to anyone the importance of your own fantasies. I am going to talk specifically about the fantasies I hold of other people. What I'll call 'true fantasies'. Fantasies of how other people, you in this instance, could behave towards me.

Some have called it a matter of image, self-image, desire, even imagination. But I want to crawl into it deeper. I want to look at someone, one person, and their standing in relation to me. Me, in some qualified future sense, though don't let the time sense lag on too long. Maybe a couple of days. I'm not that interested in distant futures, not yet anyway, though the thought is always there. At hand, one might say.

I am not purposely meaning to be obscure. One can never shift from the abstract to the specific with any ease. It's not a matter of *you*. This story, after all, is totally about you. You, who will be kissed on a later page. You, who try to live alone. You who have preoccupied my conscious hours, both asleep and awake. You who have three children. You who think that

157

maybe you might now, have always, been attracted (attractive) to men. You who I've fallen for.

FOUR SCENES LIKE REAL LIFE

Scene One. There is this person who has been out of love for almost a year. He (me) meets this guy, accidentally. It is always accidentally. At the age that this fellow is (me), he feels that the vast assaults of romantic, tragic love are thankfully over, locked in the specific age of an age previous to the age that he has now reached (meaning he's almost forty). In other words, he has reached the age when the shock of adolescent yearnings and unfulfilled desires are just annoying (that's what he prefers to think). He is middle-aged. He would rather listen to singing, blues and rock-n-roll and go to dinner with his friends of many years' standing, and then go to bed to sleep alone, masturbate occasionally (sometimes heavily) and be content in work.

Scene Two. He goes to films, predominantly films made by people he has known for years. He likes that sort of closeness, that intimacy. He goes to parties too, many, but avoids the ones which are organised to advance careers. He stops being invited to those ones because he can't avoid misbehaving, so his dinner invitations particularly do, after a while, drop off. Increasingly, he seeks out crowds. New people, he loves new people, but never eschews the old. 'Slowly his life did polarise into the old, into the new.' But that's okay. He has never been fond of the middle ground. Final versions, is how he terms the middle ground.

Scene Three. He tests. He tests every situation against his list of things to be despised or longed for. Politics (–). Poverty (–). Generosity (++). Materialism (–). Genuine unhappiness and cowardice, sometimes positive, sometimes negative.

158

Laughter (+++). Lies (--). But above everything else, he tests for idealism (++++). It had come as a profound shock to him that most people were not idealists. 'Never mind,' said his friends when he told them. 'It's a hard realisation. But most people never set out to be idealists. That's why we stick together.' And it had taken him the best part of his early life to notice this. He'd been too relaxed in his testing.

Scene Four. He gets confused by love.

We walk along the sand at Bondi Beach. It is a hot mid-day just after Xmas. It rained late this morning. The beach is remarkably clear of people but the sand is no longer wet. It feels a little like the fifties, this sparse suburban interlude, running from the waves not to get your feet wet, the sand soft here, lighter, which makes it shimmer. That sort of description.

Five lifesavers practise rescuing. Four of them carry the victim aloft, a slow measured march up the sand. The victim seems to have an erection as he's given mouth to mouth resuscitation, though this could be my imagination.

On the south side, boys try to tease crabs from between the rocks and end up frustrated, collecting tiny grey starfish that hang around the limpets and the black-and-silver-striped turban molluscs. An occasional sea anemone waits patiently for something to brush against it, then turns into a scarlet blob against the bright-green slime.

I notice there aren't any cunjevoys that squirt sea-water as you stand on them. I remember some around here years ago. They've probably gone, like the stencilled Aboriginal handprints that people remember seeing as students on excursions as late as the early sixties. Faded, vanished, built over, like the midden that Bondi once was when the Aboriginals used to come here to eat fish and yams and gaze at their nation's rock carvings. Like we come here to eat fish and chips and stare at the graffiti – DROOGIES RULE OKAY, and KEVIN LOVES AMANDA, TRUE! Like the hand prints, or is this taking comparisons too far?

There are two sites of Aboriginal rock carvings in Bondi, one in the south and one in the north in the golf course. The Waverley Council regrooved them in 1964 'to preserve their outlines'. Two weeks ago, Chips took four Yuendumu people from the Northern Territory to see these sites. Someone took a video. Like any guests they were gracious, kept their thoughts to themselves. As if they themselves were only an aftermath, diplomats in a foreign country.

———

She came back to Australia for Christmas, briefly. To Sydney. She'd been away for five years in the Middle East and they'd arranged to get together for a drink that afternoon. Neither of them said anything when he opened the door, just hugged each other. 'Let's not even mention jet lag,' she said as she walked in. 'Just give me a drink.'

'It's good to see you,' he said.

'I can't say I'm glad to be back,' she answered, walking in. 'But what I will say is, I'm glad to be away.' He poured them both a glass of champagne. 'You wouldn't believe what you have to go through to get a drink over there,' she said, looking around his lounge room. Looking at the modern Aboriginal paintings on his walls.

'They don't look too traditional painted in acrylics, do they. Still, they're nice. As paintings. I don't understand about culture anymore.

'Listen,' she said, suddenly serious. 'You know what's so weird about having been away and then coming back again? No one talks about the political anymore. Living in an international trouble spot taught me that. Not immediately, but after a time it hit me. The most anyone does now, if they've got the slightest idea about anything, is think about politics secretly. That's all. We think about it while we listen to people talk about what's happening in other countries. The places they've been to for a holiday. Blah blah. And they never come back telling you about politics. It's always about Palaces and Leather Shoes and Important Collections of ART and the funny thing that happened to them on the way to the Prado. Listen, let me tell you about the Mona Lisa, they say. I saw it. It's small, tiny. And you can't even see much behind the bullet-proof glass. Mostly all you see is a reflection of yourself looking. But that's Paris, they say. They never tell you about the beggars on the streets.

'Or the Pacific. I'm told it costs less to go to Vanuatu for a month than it does to go to Melbourne for a week. Is that true? And you come back with a reef tan from a coral beach that's located somewhere *reserved* and it's all so cheap, it's like a minute's pay. And the natives do everything with a smile. They'll even bring you off for a dollar. No wonder politics has gone underground, disappeared. It's stopped being fashionable.

'Remember, twenty years ago it was still reasonable to visit a kibbutz. Whatever else was happening in Israel, there was still the illusion of socialism, or the remnants of it, surrounding a kibbutz. The idea of a kibbutz was permeated with values, hope, the imagination of a new life. Even through the violence and the international betrayal called Zionism, a kibbutz still sounded somehow heroic. Even fifteen years ago that was the way it seemed. Even to women.

'That's the difference two decades makes in these peace-strewn times. We've got used to the warless murder of insignificant strangers. We no longer even watch as we sit by our TV sets, overcome by a kind of thoughtlessness, a larger-than-life alcohol-infused mist, a sip-by-sip confusion. Talking, so opinionated, and everyone so quick to condemn. But no one to blame, not directly. And we hear someone sitting next to us saying, of course people get killed throughout the world. That's only natural, in places far away where law and order have broken down. Or we think that's what they've said.' As he refills her glass, she says, 'I'm sorry. Living with war gets to you after a while. But fuck it. People still visit these places, you know. And surprisingly they don't see any dead. It's as if the newspapers back home exaggerate the mayhem by picturing it and concentrating it into seven paragraphs which then turn out to look like lies.

'It's become harder to integrate happiness. In theory it should be feasible. But smiling and drinking champagne can only be possible if you ignore the process, see and feel nothing except some kind of distilled essence, a higher plane, if you like.' She laughs at the allusion. 'That sounds a bit silly, doesn't it. Reducing everything down to drinking champagne.'

'Pour yourself another one,' he says and she laughs, pouring herself another glass which bubbles over.

She told him all this on her return from Iraq, very stridently, very passionately, as if, after five years, she had to get something very private off her chest. He never really understood why she had left Australia to return to a war zone, even though she had been brought up there, called it home. And she'd chosen to live on the border, quite in viewing distance of Iran. It seemed more normal when she told him that the government paid women money to cover themselves. 'So that when they look at us through binoculars from the other side and they see all these women dressed in chadors, they'll think that we've become fundamentalists and so won't bomb us. Only educated or very rich women make a point of wearing western clothes, as a protest.' He knew better than to ask her which she wore.

We sit on the rocks overlooking Tamarama Bay, the two people I live with and me. It is a Sunday afternoon walk, a bond that joins us. And then the rocks, the pounding waves, the solitude affects us.

Di stands on the rocks closest to the waves. Geoff standing further away looking out over the Pacific.

He looks out to New Caledonia, the Solomon Islands, Samoa. He is on an island, Australia, but the island he stands on is smaller, a coral atoll concentrated with culture. Kanaky.

She is somewhere else. She is in the outback, travelling six or eight or twelve hours on a dusty track by car or flying in precariously low over layers of red desert and lush welcomings. To a festival in Barunga or a feast in Utopia.

One of them hears fishing parties in canoes, past the breakers, in the dusk, singing.

The other's singing voices are harsher – spinifex singing, the tapping of branches and the need to wander.

But for me it is just the sea. And you and me, boys again. And I put my arm around you and solemnly ask, like a twelve-year-old, 'If you had to, if you really had to choose, would you rather eat poo or die?'

And we both agree to die.

PLEASURE

She loved sex. That is my strongest memory of her. Sex, reading and painting. My passions, she called them.

'So strange, that. After almost sixty-five years, they're the only things that can stir me still, can make me feel visionary, fortunate, I should say almost happy again.'

'Friendship?' she replies, her eyes sparkling, alive to the possibilities of my question. 'Without people there can be nothing. No art, nothing. But you should know this. People are a precondition. It is only through them that you can ever begin to find the essentials. Otherwise everything just deteriorates into aesthetics. Oh, but I am forgetting myself. I forget that my talk is the talk of an aged woman – I won't say old, not yet. Yes, one must always ask questions. You reminded me just then that at your age I too was still in love with love. *Amour*!' Her smile causes more lines on her already over-wrinkled face, but still handsome.

'Sex is my first memory of you,' I say, which causes her to laugh out loud and hold onto my elbow and say, 'That was years ago. You were still a child. And look at you now. Just look at you.' She makes a fist and gestures at time, as if saluting it while cursing.

'I will tell you something. Thinking. That has always been my real love. You can never do it by yourself, always with other people. Always. Everything else is . . . philosophy. There are too many philosophers, who needs them. There's too much of everything. You'll realise this. It clouds what is essential. Do you still find me cryptic? You said that to me one time, oh, years ago. You've probably forgotten.'

'I don't remember that.' She nods at my forgetfulness, losing herself in this reminder of other times and rubs the ageing loose skin on the back of her hand. As if to make something happen. Something spiritual.

'I don't regret anything,' she adds, rather forcefully. And then, quickly, 'But tell me about yourself. I hear bits and pieces, you know, gossip. But I want you to tell me. Are you still a poet?'

I have to laugh. 'I don't know.' Here is a woman who held me when I was two months old and I shat in her lap, asking me if I'm still a poet.

'I understand,' she says finally. 'There are things that one must always keep to oneself. It's like asking someone, but what do you love?'

'Do you still love caviar?' I ask. That makes her look at me. How can I describe that look? It is the look of a co-conspirator, a look that can only come of age and trust, a profound response to something that sounds trivial.

'But how could you know that? I haven't eaten any for years.' And then, 'How indiscreet one often is in life. And you know about this too? You must. My only real, absolute vice! My dearest one, and you've known of it all this time? After all this time I stand discovered, revealed in all my shame!' Whispering, she adds, 'I do love caviar. It is, how shall I say, my saviour.'

Having acknowledged her secret, she takes my elbow again, moves closer and says, 'But how can you know this vice of mine? You can't have guessed it.' She stares at me and knits her eyebrows, waiting for the answer. 'Tell me. I can't recall.'

'Munich,' I say, playfully.

'Ah, the bath,' she says. 'Now it is all clear.' Reminded, the past returns.

'You know, in life, often the most awful, truly horrid moments, when you think you can never live through the times you're going through, seem later, looking back, like so much shit. Rubbish. The stories, the people.' For a moment she looks ancient, then, recovering, she livens up.

'Munich, you can't imagine. A little flat, pokey, small – and we were rich, you know. Rain outside, cold like nothing, not like cold in Melbourne. Bitter cold. And I'd sneak in, alone, and I'd run a bath. A beautiful deep ceramic bath, dark green, like the sea at night. Imagine me! Door locked. Depressed something awful. Standing there shivering, the steam rising from the water and there was I, I can say this to you, you won't mind.' She quickly checks my adulthood. 'Nude. Totally naked except for an old spoon, like the spoons we had in the migrant camps, big and heavy, and a pound, *one whole pound* of the best Sturgeon caviar.'

No longer reticent, she continues, 'For all I knew or cared, the whole world could have been being wiped out outside my bathroom and I couldn't have cared. Not then. Certainly not. Nothing and no one was going to intrude on this.

'The first spoonful! After the first three spoonfuls, the grief, the darkness, you know, the calamity of your broken life slowly lifts its shroud. Even though things looked better, you knew of course that it was transient. But the bath and the caviar, spoon after spoon, made the feeling permanent for the moment. So I ate. More. Another spoonful, that's all that mattered. That *moment*. Gobbling away at those fish eggs. I only did it twice – they were the only times I could afford it.'

We sit, reflecting on our own temptations and each other's vices.

'You introduced me to my first caviar, you know,' I interrupt. 'I was seventeen and you came around with *malasol*.'

'Yes, smuggled in, I remember. I carried it in myself. It was – don't remind me – it was someone's birthday . . . No, it's gone.'

(A family dinner. Lots of kisses and noise and a little tin of grey pearly comfort. 'Open it,' she said to me.)

'You told me to try it. Don't you remember?'

'Too long ago.'

'You turned to me and whispered, don't be so well behaved. Be a pig, but never nibble. Spoon it in! Later you told me about Munich.'

'Oh! Lilya's birthday, of course.'

'When I'd finished all the caviar you said, you see, there was enough for everyone. Next time it'll be someone else's turn to be greedy. You've had your turn, so you won't mind. But if you do, that means it's time to run a bath, lock the door and do it secretly. That's what you said.'

'I can imagine that I did, because it's true. Whatever you do alone is no one else's business.'